AF486700

Watch Party

Lancaster Cooney

ANUCI PRESS

Tanuci69@gmail.com

First paperback edition 2026

Anuci Press edition 2026

www.anuci-press.com

Cover Design by Darin Overholser

ISBN 979-8-9936803-3-0 (paperback)

ISBN 979-8-9936803-2-3 (eBook)

This one's for Molly, Dee Dee and Bill

(And all the legends of Anderson Township)

Calm Jeffrey

We sat in a pot circle in Stanley Kemper's two-car garage, sophomore year. David Trumner rolled two joints on an old wooden coffee table and sent them out in opposite directions. David was a long hair who exclusively wore tie-dyes. We called him *The Gizzard King* on account of his similarities to the late Jim Morrison. Not the young model, but the hairy, bloated version that died in a bathtub. Adrian Bowler once referred to him as *Jim Morrison's sexless little brother* and a group of about ten of us nearly pissed our pants. Sam Bently sat next to him and hit the joints incessantly, claiming, *"Damn it! I didn't mean to hit that!"* after each rip, as *OK Computer* played on an old CD boombox.

At one point Julie Derringer ended up with both joints. Honker of a nose on that girl. She'd have it whittled down in her early twenties while the doctor was in there fixing a deviated septum, but it made no matter; we still saw her for what she was. Caroline was Julie's friend from Mt. Notre Dame Academy, but she didn't seem uppity. Then, as likely now, teenage boys referred to the girls of Mt. Notre Dame as *the hoes on the hill*, but then, surely as it remains to this day, was based more on depraved yearning than any sort of statistical proof. She was basic and pretty and had these big, beautiful brown eyes the size of fishbowls and this cutesy way of tucking her hair back behind an ear that reminded me of the roost of a really graceful hawk. But the main thing that struck me was the way her face seemed to naturally hold a smile. As though the flesh had settled the way the foundation of an old house might.

I was your quintessential suburban teen with moderately effective good looks, deceptive height, and a socially acceptable wardrobe consisting of a t-shirt, jeans, and a well-worn pair of Vans. So, basically speaking, she was out of my league.

Julie offered her one of the joints and she plucked it from her hand in one hurried motion, swiping and attaining the little bastard before taking two magnanimous rips.

"Word on the street is he broke the teacher's cheekbone," Julie said. "Blood everywhere."

"Yeah, well, that's firsthand knowledge from an unreliable source," Kemper followed. "And there was no blood. That's all bullshit."

"Well, is the teacher back to school?" she asked. Which was a legitimate argument. All the teachers, not to mention Mr. Kimbi, the superintendent, had been on somewhat of a public relations tour in the weeks following the incident. Bringing in counselors from Lower Your Flag to speak with anyone who might be feeling uneasy. But the overall message was that Mrs. Cummings was doing just fine and resting comfortably at home. They also presented the option of sending her a get-well message should anyone be so inclined.

"She's on medical leave," Kemper said sheepishly.

"Yeah. For a broken cheekbone."

"*Hearsay*," Kemper exclaimed, standing and shushing Julie by plugging one of the joints into her tiny mouth. Kemper was handsome in a proper way. Type of teen with the physique of a swimmer and thick brown hair that looked fashionable, even when messy. Only one of us who might have gone on to attend an Ivy League school.

"Just tell them, man," Trumner said. "You're the one he told."

"Yeah, but Kohlhepp's full of shit, man. Thus, unreliable."

"Your mom's unreliable," Trumner said.

"She's always *cum* through for me," Bently followed, leaning back into one of the two sofas we were sitting on, eyes on the precipice of sleep. Bently was small in stature, with thin blonde hair that came down in straight bangs. He wore expensive clothing from Abercrombie & Fitch and glasses folks referred to as *serial killer* glasses. Mainly, on account of what that dude in Milwaukee did in the 1980s. Bently was a smart kid with surprising wit. Built to unleash zinger after zinger, when not nearly comatose.

"Leave Cindy out of this, dickheads," Kemper said in a playful attempt to defend his mom's honor. "She's a saint." Which made the girls start to giggle and us guys look around proudly, as though we were really putting on a show.

"Allison Elam corroborated the whole story. You just don't like what you heard about your old buddy, old pal. Afraid he might scurry down the street and climb in your window at night."

"That ganja's gone to your head, kid," Kemper said, leaning over and jabbing Trumner in the meat of his belly. Trumner took the blow by doing that thing where you sort of tighten your abdomen and let out a quick exhalation of laughter. That was the thing you had to give

Trumner—even when being sort of an ass, he had this likeable charm.

"Wait," Caroline said, walking over to the open mouth of the garage door. We'd made the decision to keep the other door closed to hide our transgressions from the neighbors, i.e., drinking and smoking. "Which house are we looking at again?"

"Top of the street. Dead center," Trumner confirmed, closing an eye as though looking down the scope of a rifle and pointing with a joint wedged between his index and thumb. "Kemper and Bausch here used to be friends with the kid, until he went all weird."

Kemper's house sat at the bottom of a cul-de-sac on Candlemaker Drive, with the back of the house sloping down to where the yard eventually met the woods and Clough Creek. Candlemaker was lined with similar model homes built in the booming housing market of the 1980s. The house Trumner pointed to ran horizontally to the top of the street where Candlemaker met Spinning Wheel. On snow days in our early childhood, we'd spent countless hours zipping down Kemper's backyard, abandoning our sleds midway down the hill, relegating our empty sleds to crash through the woods and into the creek bed. On more than a few occasions, kids tried to prove their worth by bravely, or *not* so bravely, staying aboard their sleds too long, only to find themselves among the rocks and branches. Faces scratched. Winter coats punctured to the point that the stuffing poked though like little pieces of popcorn, and an occasional snow hat was snatched clean from head by brush and branch. There was little judgment in those days save for the nuances of immature friendships.

"He didn't go *all weird*," I said. "He has a condition."

"Yeah, if being fucked in the head can be considered a condition," Trumner followed.

"*Really, dude?*" Kemper said, noticing the disgust on Caroline's face when she turned back to look at the group. "Have a little couth, would ya?"

"Did he really talk in tongues?" Caroline asked.

"Not tongues," I told her, taking the opportunity to join her where she stood at the threshold of the garage. "It was more like a bunch of people talking all at once."

We stared out at the house, the lawn overwrought with weed and clover. Miner Kent was tending to the upkeep of the property as an act of charity for a while. Most people saw Mrs. Tarkin as sort of a tragic figure. Husband who up and walked out on them. Messed-up kid. Doing all she could to make ends meet working as a clerk at Kramer's Market. Quiet type. Didn't so much as look up when she rang you out at the register. And always mumbling beneath her breath when stocking shelves. Claimed she was quoting scripture. But Miner Kent had long since hung up his endeavors toward generosity. It was rumored he was bitten. Never fully verified, but Jodie Kline's mom, who was a nurse over at St. Elizabeth, told her Miner Kent was in for a tetanus shot and some antibiotics. And folks reported seeing him wearing a bandage upon his right forearm around the time the incident was rumored to have happened.

"Shut the fuck up, Bausch. You weren't even there, man," Trumner said.

"Talked to Allison. It's true."

"Clearly you all have a hard-on for this Allison chick."

"Don't be jealous, Julie. It's not becoming," Kemper said, to which Julie responded with a bony middle finger and flirtatious tongue. It was weird, even her tongue was pointy. No rounded edges to the girl at all.

"Allison's not one to add fabric," I said.

"So?" Caroline asked. "What'd she say?"

"She said it was like his voice overlapped. Reminded her of when we used to say The Pledge of Allegiance in grade school." There was fear during the retelling of what she witnessed. She visibly shook and seemed hesitant, as though sharing the account might somehow cause something similar to happen to her simply by talking about it. She sat on the bleachers in the gym after class was over and nearly everyone else had cleared out. Staring at nothing. That's when I asked if she was okay.

"Gross," Julie said.

"That's just it. Allison said there was something about it that made her feel kind of sick. Said it was like his throat and lungs were filled with fluid."

Right on cue, Trumner unleashed a juicy burp smelling of Mt. Dew, and Julie and Kemper covered their mouths and pinched their noses. It was then that he made the horrendous decision to blow his personal chemtrail directly into the face of a sleeping, widemouthed Sam Bently, who subsequently gagged a bit but never completely woke up.

"*Sick*," Julie exclaimed.

"Dude, uncalled for," Kemper laughed.

But Trumner had no aversion to negative attention. It was all welcome with him.

Caroline walked back into the garage and sat on one of the two sofas Kemper's grandmother had gifted the family upon her passing. Kemper was able to talk his parents into letting him put them out in the garage along with the coffee table and vomit-colored plush carpet to provide us a proper hangout. We spent the better part of summer and most of fall sitting out in the garage, giving each other hell.

But that was the first time any girls had stopped by. And not for lack of trying.

"Allison said she was coming back from the restroom when she heard some sort of growl."

"*Bullshit*," Trumner said.

"No, that's right. Exactly what Kohlhepp told me. It was a growl."

"*Oh, come on, man.*"

"*Dude*, you told us to tell you," I snapped. "So shut the fuck up."

After saying that, I inadvertently looked Caroline's way, where she was both smiling and leaning forward in anticipation of what I had to say. Sam Bently snored aggressively, doing one of those type deals where you momentarily snort yourself awake, which caused us to branch off into momentary laughter.

"She was coming up the steps over by the new science wing and said Mrs. Cummings was right there on the landing trying to comfort Adam."

"Adam?" Caroline asked, clearly hearing his name for the first time.

"Yeah," I told her. "Adam Tarkin." *The mental case. The tragic soul. The possessed boy.* It just depended on who was talking about him, and which story they were telling. Because there were many. "Allison said she was just sort of rubbing his back as he was trying to catch his breath. Apparently he was vomiting. Again, she said his lungs sounded compromised. As though he'd aspirated or something."

"Why?" Julie asked. "Was he sick?"

"Not sure. Jamie Lipton was in class with him that morning and said all was normal. He was quiet, but kid's always quiet. Hardly says a word, honestly. Mr. Victor tried to make an ass out of him in World History by directing all questions his way, but Adam just stared down at his desk."

"Kid's fucked up," Trumner added.

"Pot callin' the kettle black there, fella," Kemper chided.

"Fair," Trumner agreed.

"Anyway, not long after she walked up on the two, Allison said he fuckin' flipped. Next thing she knew, Mrs. Cummings ended up face down on the tile, and Kohlhepp, Mr. Crawford, and Mr. Nantz were trying to subdue him."

"Kohlhepp said he was strong as shit. And Mr. Crawford's a wiry motherfucker. Collegiate wrestler back in the day."

"Shit. I bet Kohlhepp stood there and watched like a pussy," Trumner said.

"Part that got me was how Allison described him talking. Said his neck sort of jutted away from his body at an impossible angle and his face kept going back and forth between Kohlhepp and the teachers. Taunting them. Getting right up in their faces. Slow and methodical. Mumbled something about Mr. Nantz's mother and mocked Kohlhepp's manhood. Personal shit."

"Accurate shit," Trumner said. "I have P.E. with Kohlhepp."

"Allison said he just sort of got worn down after that."

"*Wow*," Caroline responded.

"*You think this is cool?*" Julie playfully accused Caroline.

"Oh, I don't know. Maybe a little fascinating, right?"

"Probably on drugs," Bently added, still slouched behind them on the sofa.

"Oh, look who decided to join us," Trumner said, leaning back and placing his head on Bently's bony little shoulder. Snuggling in.

"Would never leave you, big guy," Bently told him, pulling Trumner into an intimate embrace and placing a kiss on his puffy head.

"Hey, don't forget about me," Kemper said before jumping onto the laps of our pals and insisting I join. "*Get in here, Bauschy…Get your lil ass in here!*" Which I did, reluctantly. More so out of discomfort than any want to participate in the melee. Caroline seemed to enjoy the way our group operated, and though I couldn't always relate to them as a whole, I was grateful to be a part of it.

Just then a loud *honk* stole our attention. We all got up and walked out onto the driveway as a maroon-colored Pontiac Bonneville pulled into the cul-de-sac and stopped with the passenger side facing us. Nathan Dufour reached over and worked the window down manually. Now, by maroon, it should be noted that the overall body of the car was maroon, but the hood and paneling along the back wheel-well was more of a beige-ish color. Likely pulled from Mooney's Salvage and Auto Repair to make up the whole. Trumner wasted no time making a mockery of our longtime friend.

"Doof. Doof. love the car, man. Really killing it in life."

And we all fucking lost it. Sometimes, even when being sort of an asshole, Trumner's comic timing was irrefutable. Dufour flipped him the bird and waved the group closer. "Gonna grab a few sixers. What do you all want?" he asked, unable to bring his gaze up to meet the pretty young girls in our company. A litany of requests followed, ranging from PBR and Coors Original to Jager, Boone's Farm, and Grey Goose—the latter of which was requested by Julie in order to present a high-end option and directly heighten her social status—each of us going elbow-deep into our pockets to retrieve cash. "Whoa, whoa, whoa. Wait a minute. Who's goin' with?"

"I'll go," Caroline said without hesitation, which caused me to mumble beneath my breath, "*I fuckin' love you.*" Dufour was taken aback as he nervously reached a thick arm across the passenger seat and fumbled with the tiny lock knob. Dufour was beefy, massive actually, which only aided his ability to purchase beverages at an early age. Another aspect that abetted such activities was his ability to grow a serious beard. Not the prepubescent curlicues the rest of us were left to work with, but an all-out lumberjack type deal.

"*Shotgun,*" Caroline announced, as I made a play at chivalry by opening the passenger door. Presenting a sweeping hand that was intended to say *my lady*. She smiled and purposefully brought her face close to mine as she ducked into the seat. Close enough that I could feel her breath on my cheek. This beautiful young creature that was, at least momentarily, paying attention to me. The rest of the group receded into the distance as we pulled away. I looked out the back window to witness Trumner toss an arm over Julie's shoulder only to have her maneuver out of it with a spin and walk away. Kemper shook his head at Trumner's juvenile attempt before stamping his fists down into the front pockets of his jeans and following her.

Trumner stood there with his palms facing up, seemingly saying *What'd I do?* as Dufour ran the stop sign at the top of the street and hung a right toward the front of the neighborhood.

As we pulled past Tarkin's house, I found myself reminiscing about our old friend. Not the teenage outcast we'd come to know, but the one me and Kemper walked through the creeks with on summer days or sat on the front stoop of Emerson's Bakery with eating sprinkled donuts on Saturday mornings. The kid who used to be funny. And he was. He really used to be somebody. Same Adam Tarkin who showed us our first pair of titties in one of his father's *Playboys* from the top shelf of the basement closet. The one with Drew Barrymore wearing a studded choker in a swimming pool, arms raised, titties pulled taut. A young boy's dream. Same Adam Tarkin who was able to work amazing shapes across his bedroom wall with only the aid of a flashlight pinned in place between chest and chin. Putting the backs of his hands together and arching his fingers just in front of the light. And that was it, *magic*. Manipulating his hands into the shadow of a rabbit, or a bird taking flight. Hell, even an elephant. That one was wild. The palm of his left hand facing the floor while subsequently pointing his middle and ring fingers down and side by side to portray the trunk. All the while, contorting his pinky and index fingers to depict prominent ivory tusks. "That's legit," Kemper would tell him. "Real impressive, Tarkin."

But the one that always got us was the old man in the hat. To look at Adam's fists, one atop the other, you would hardly figure it possible how the shadow contained so much detail and depth. Almost seemed alive. But when you zeroed in on the shadow, it was clearly an old man wearing a beaten old hat. Type a bum might wear in an old movie. And that was a marvel to behold. Something that Kemper and I could not quite wrap our heads around, the way Adam began to manipulate his features, making him scrunch his face and talk. Only, it was as though Adam was sort of throwing his voice, never seeming to move a muscle. And the voice didn't come off as muffled the way it often does when folks are doing ventriloquism. The old man introduced himself as *Calm Jeffrey* and he could smell our fear. The first few occasions were your typical spiders, ghosts, or dying in a fire, but then the shadow began speaking of other things, things he could never know. Things Adam could never know. The slow monotone voice Adam used to depict Calm Jeffrey getting inside our heads. Rattling the very structure of our brains, saying, "*I know...I know...*" turning to face me with a nursery rhyme sort of singsong, *"Scottie Mills, the mailman, crawling through your head..."*

"Stop it, Tarkin!"

"Scottie Mills, the mailman, climbing up your bed..."

"I said fuckin' *stop it,* Tarkin!" Kemper hollered, seeing the overwhelming fear on my face.

"...it was a car on Blushing Avenue, somebody said...Struck and killed the mailman, now he's DEAD! DEAD! DEAD!"

Adam stopped, not by choice but rather force after Kemper crawled out of his sleeping bag and punched the flashlight out from under his chin.

"Enough!"

And then the bedroom went dark. All three of us were breathing as though we'd just hoofed it up Round Bottom Road to make curfew. Only, something else was breathing. Soft. Sardonic. At the very spot Adam cast Calm Jeffrey upon the wall.

It was a story that went unnoticed by most, but for me it would become somewhat of a haunting core memory. I'd first read about it in my dad's newspaper, drawn to the headline that made a play on the common phrase *Out for Delivery.* Even at such a young age I'd found it to be distasteful, but the news was a diabolical and competitive industry. Later that evening, I caught a segment on

Channel 9 News. Jenna Kennedy stood on the corner of Blushing Avenue and Harlow Road as snow speckled her straight brown hair. She was pretty, though wore too much makeup and delivered the report in a discerning and pretentious voice. Words that she'd likely practiced aloud as the camera crew set up their equipment. Telling the tale of how a drunk driver in a truck, one of those big dudes, big enough to haul a colosseum, had pinned Scottie Mills against a guardrail, severing his body in half where he would die at the scene. "No shit," I mumbled to the obviousness of such a comment, snickering to myself. And then came the face of the man upon the television with the headline at the bottom of the screen reading *Beloved husband, father, and mailman*. Well, that was just too much. I felt instant guilt for the insensitive remark and nonchalance with which I'd brushed off the man's death. In short, I felt like a complete piece of shit. It would be that same face that would haunt my nightmares, both sleeping and while awake. Same face that scuttled across my bedroom carpet and latched onto my covers, causing me to pull them tightly beneath my chin, unknowingly assisting the upper torso of Scottie Mills up onto my bed.

And then there was the incident at Kramer's Market one Saturday afternoon while shopping with my mom. She pushed the cart ahead as I was hijacked by a smorgasbord of ice cream in the freezer section. I was reaching in for a carton of peanut butter chip when something caught my eye. Reminded me of one of those wooden snakes I'd begged my parents for at a gift shop in Gatlinburg. Type of deal where you hold the tail and can manipulate the body of the snake to slither in midair out in front of you. Just the slightest movement of the wrist and that dude was slithering. It was a movement similar to that that I'd seen turn the corner at the end of the aisle. And just that quickly, I knew what it was. *Who* it was! As I stepped backward, retraced my steps to the beginning of the freezer aisle, and hesitantly peeked around the corner of the next aisle over, I knew exactly what I would see. Scottie Mills the mailman pawing his way down the aisle, palms slapping against the tile floor as his vertebrae drug in a sloppy, bony tail behind him. *Rattling. Actually rattling in his wake.* The man's face looking down at the floor until he heard me gasp. And then it was all-encompassing. Scottie Mills crawling as fast as inhumanly possible, directly toward me, screaming that horrible scream indicative of someone on the cusp of a terrible death. And then my mother was there in front of me, shaking me back to reality, crouched and pulling me toward her in a protective way. Random store clerk looking down on us in disgust.

"I don't really drink much," Caroline turned and confessed.

Through the front window of the liquor store Dufour could be seen retrieving six packs of beer and cradling them within the nooks of his thick inner elbows. All his movements were sporadic and confused, traipsing back through aisles trying to locate vodka, whiskey, and wine. Even from the distance where we sat, his face clearly registered that of annoyed desperation.

"Yeah, me either," I said, clarifying that I also didn't really drink. Which was true. I didn't care much for it and was still very much of that age where the fear of vomiting was a paralyzing force. "We could always pour them out when no one's looking?"

"Deal," she said, reaching a petite little hand back to shake on it. It was cold, but smooth. Whereas mine was more on the lineage of calloused and clammy. Clammy due to nerves and calloused on account of my recent endeavors toward lifting weights. I wasn't a twig by any means, but there was little to no definition to my physique, something I'd become a bit insecure about in the last year or so. But I was tall enough for my age. Never really understood why my parents' friends always saw the need to point it out, though. Always saying things such as *Boy's growing like a weed* or *You've really sprouted since we last saw you, young man*. I was just beginning to learn what a social advantage it was to simply have some height on your side.

"You know what I feel bad about?"

"What?"

"Tonight. I kind of feel bad about tonight. He was my friend. Not the last couple of years, but at one point, ya know? Guess I feel sort of gross watching him like he's some sort of sideshow."

"What happened?" she asked, and then quickly followed with, "If you don't mind my asking?"

"No. Of course not. And I don't mean to make you feel bad. I guess it's just weighing on me a little."

"Well, I'm glad to be hanging out with you. If that means anything? I saw you once at Kings Island during the summer. Almost said hi, but wasn't sure you'd recognize me."

"What? No? Seriously? And I would have totally recognized you. Remember seeing you at the game when we played Cov Cath."

"Ugh, those guys are a bunch of assholes."

"Yeah, they beat our asses."

We both smiled, momentarily caught up in one simple moment in time.

"Encephalitis," I finally said.

"What?"

"Tarkin. It was encephalitis."

"And what exactly is that?"

"Yeah, I didn't really know either. It's when your brain swells. They weren't sure what caused it. Could have been any number of things. Said his immune system was actually attacking his brain. His mom found him in the bathroom. Woke up to a thud in the middle of the night. Not loud, just consistent. *Thud...thud...thud...* Said he was sitting on the bathroom floor, sort of cradling the toilet like people do when vomiting. Only, he was resting the side of his head against the toilet seat, every once in a while lifting it up and slamming it down, causing the seat to bounce and rattle. Saying over and over again, *My pizza hurts. My pizza hurts.*"

"Why was he saying that?"

"Guess that's all his brain could put together?"

"That's awful."

"It was bad. He was in the hospital for eight weeks. On a breathing tube. My mom took me to see him. Thought it might help. You know, to hear my voice or something?"

"Was he in a coma?"

"I honestly don't know," I said, completely unaware of the outward trauma I was exhibiting until I felt a hand come down on my knee. "Then, one day, he woke up."

The driver's side door popped open, and Dufour began unloading a small grocery cart of beer and bottles of Jager, Boone's Farm, and Grey Goose. "*Dinner is served*," he announced from outside the car, his enormous arms transporting the beer, wine, and booze my and Caroline's way. We found it comical, as he looked decapitated, simply reaching into the cart and handing off each item blindly with the expectation we would accept. Caroline playfully hesitated to take the bottle of Jager which led to Dufour shaking the bottle as though saying, *Take the damn thing, would ya?* which had us cracking up. "Hilarious. A couple of comedians."

The pleather seat of the Bonneville groaned as he eased back down into the car. He kept a handle on a six pack of Coors Original and broke three of them away from the plastic rings. "*To Tarkin*," he said, cracking his open and offering the can up in tribute, pausing and waiting for us to follow suit. We looked to each other before snapping the tabs of our cans and raising them in solidarity.

"*To Tarkin*," we said.

"Poor bastard," Dufour mumbled.

We drove back to the house listening to that Natalie Imbruglia song that seemed to be playing all day on the radio and over Muzak in the grocery store. The one where she found herself so torn up over a guy that she somehow ended up naked on the floor. Real piece of shit song but inundated the airwaves back then. Caroline looked back, playfully lip syncing to the tune as I pretended to pour the remainder of my beer down onto the floor mat behind Dufour's seat. Those big, beautiful eyes of hers making my heart palpitate in accordance with my excitement. No other care in the world.

Curfew Is a Broken Clock

I felt it somewhat despicable when people found entertainment in other people's tragedy, yet there we were. And what made it worse was that the adults in the neighborhood began to blatantly gather at the Ellisons' up the street, not more than twenty yards from the Tarkins' residence. Deploying soccer chairs, sipping wine coolers and cheap beer, forming a sort of semi-circle that opened up to the event that was rumored to soon take place across the street. Maddy Holt walked around with a tray of sausage and cheese, those in the group giving thanks before stabbing portions onto their plates with tiny colored toothpicks. Mr. Ellison pridefully wheeled a Weber Genesis I grill out onto the driveway, causing Mike

Adams and Alan Bremer to walk over and stare at the thing as though it was some sort of rare sports car or something.

Kemper and I were blindsided on the way home from school the day Mr. Ellison purchased the grill, forced to listen to a thirty-minute dissertation on the nuances of the unit. "Went with the chocolate hood on account of our shutters," Mr. Ellison said, pointing over his shoulder with a set of matching tongs to draw attention to the shutters. "The wife wanted cherry, but I went ahead and made an executive decision. And she's coming around to it." We learned of the Genesis I's output ability of 36,000 BTUs and the luxury of having 543 square inches of total cooking area, which broke down to approximately 423 square inches of primary cooking space along with the complementary 120-square-inch warming rack. "Which is nice," not to mention the three long-lasting, stainless-steel burners and dual-purpose thermometer capable of reading the temperature of the cooking chamber or doneness load.

"What exactly do you mean by *load*?" Kemper made the mistake of joking. A joke that of course was completely lost on Mr. Ellison, sailing over his head and out into the ether.

"Comes down to one's preference, really, with one-hundred-twenty degrees indicative of rare, one-thirty, medium, and so on." As he said this, he crossed his arms in a focused manner. "You know, doneness load."

"*Load. Got it*," Kemper responded, as if he gave a shit. Mimicking actually shooting a load all over Mr. Ellison's back when the man crouched down to display the grease management system. Which apparently reduced flareups and was of absolutely no interest to either of us.

My parents never really cared much for the Ellison's on account of Mr. Ellison's constant partying and inability to properly venture into adulthood and Mrs. Ellison's unwillingness to acknowledge that things were less than hunky-dory. Mr. Ellison was the consummate jock turned high school baseball coach, while Mrs. Ellison made an income selling high-end makeup and novelty devices that were left about the house in a not-so-discreet manner. Joe Mulvihill claimed that while over there with his mom, he found what appeared to be a little rubbery elephant riding a silver rocket down in the living room sofa. Said the thing stank to high hell and buzzed about when the end was twisted. Never let on to his mom that he came across the item and ended up stuffing it back between the cushions and immediately rushing to the bathroom for a hand scrub. Sounded slightly horrific.

Since our return from the liquor store, Julie and Kemper had formed some sort of an unspoken connection, standing close together and taking every opportunity to touch one another. Constant eye contact. Unwarranted laughter. In other words, super flirty. So much so that Julie had turned the color of an eraser and Kemper inadvertently clenched his jaw to enunciate his masseter muscle. Dude had an epic jawline, though was still not vain in the way most kids are at that age.

"Seems sort of disrespectful, doesn't it?" Julie asked.

"As opposed to what we're doin'?" Trumner followed.

"Are your parents up there?" Caroline asked.

"Nah," Kemper said. "Not their cup. My dad's out of town and my mom works nights at Anderson Commons."

His mom worked with the elderly for as long as I could remember. Claimed to be drawn to their honesty and wisdom and the way their mouths seemed concave when absent of dentures. "They're just so sweet," she'd always say. Kemper's mom was welcoming and kind and had that innate way of calling you *honey* or *sweetie* without it coming off as disingenuous. And I'm certain she'd brought a lot of those old bags at Anderson Commons copious amounts of peace in their waning years. She was also pretty good looking for a mom, and little did Kemper know that when we were making mom jokes, we were all secretly acting out those fantasies in our minds. At least,

I know I was, and I was far and away among the more civilized of our classmates.

"What time's your mom get home?" Julie asked.

"*Be a lady,*" Kemper demanded. "*You can't sleep over.*"

"Oh, you wish," she said, laughing and turning even more red. "Besides, I have curfew, genius."

"Curfew is a broken clock," Kemper responded.

Caroline smiled at me and playfully rolled her eyes. I smiled back. Sam Bently hit the joints one more time each and shortly thereafter began berating Trumner for passing them his way. "*Seriously, man. You're doin' me no good. I don't need to hit those.*" Dufour and Trumner stood over an empty garbage can that Kemper's dad used to dump grass and weeds. They each punched a slightly overgrown thumbnail through the thin aluminum of a beer can before taking them to the dome.

"Seriously, fellas," Kemper reminded them. "No evidence. You clean up anything you spill."

It was then that Caroline heard the bell ring for the first time. Walking up to the open mouth of the garage in time to see Mrs. Tarkin ringing a decent-sized farm bell mounted to the brick of their front porch. She rang it exactly three times before turning and walking back into the house. Julie stepped up beside Caroline and asked, "What's that all about?"

"Bitch is crazy," Trumner said.

"Don't know," I told them. "Started doin' that a few months back."

"Yeah," Kemper chimed in. "She came out frantically ringing that bell the day Tarkin attacked Mrs. Cummings. Neighbors had to call nine-one-one and everything. Totally lost her shit, as if she knew something was happening with Adam."

"No way," Julie said.

"It's true," I attested.

"Turns out he had a seizure. Hardly able to use the left side of his body," Kemper added.

"You are all so full of shit," Julie said, walking back over and pouring herself some Grey Goose. "I don't know what the hell to believe."

Caroline stuck to our plan of pouring while the others were occupied. Slipping a full beer beneath crossed arms for me to casually empty in the bush just outside the open door, with me returning the empty can to her hand directly after the pour. It felt good, the two of us working together. Our own private accord.

"*What the fuck?*" Trumner said, turning his back and immediately beginning to clean up beer cans and hide bottles of booze behind power tools and other random items in the garage. "*Bently, cover those joints, man.*" But

Bently was too far gone. Julie and Caroline instantly went to work on him, taking the joints and stabbing them out in an ashtray before covering them with a giant Tupperware bowl. Kemper hit the fan just as I caught sight of Mr. Ellison walking down the sidewalk with a plate of meat. *"Bently, look alive, you fuck."*

Mr. Ellison wore an Anderson High School baseball cap that seemed capable of splitting at the seams due to the pressure of his oversized melon. There was a secretive joke amongst his players that went something like this: "Would you rather have a million dollars or Coach Ellison's hat full of pennies?" He wore shorts, though the evenings were getting rather cold, with white socks and Nike slip-on sandals. A look that never quite got off the ground, unbeknownst to him. The girls worked in a unified manner to stand in front of Bently and sort of shroud him from sight, as Kemper put on his best *responsible young man* act before heading Mr. Ellison off on the driveway. I took two shots of body spray to my t-shirt and jeans before walking out to support him.

"*Mr. Ellison,*" Kemper said. "What have we got here?"

"Figured you kids might be hungry," said the overgrown, redheaded man-child. "What with your mom and dad always working." The Ellison's, as well as much of the neighborhood, were constantly taking shots at my and

Kemper's parents on account of their rare participation in social gatherings. Both of whom found the hierarchy and high school-like mentality of them all absolutely unbearable.

Kemper acknowledged the dig with a grin and a head-cock to the side and decided to take the high road. "*Really generous of you.*" Mr. Ellison extended a plate of burgers and bratwurst as well as those little packets of condiments they toss into your bag at fast food restaurants. "*Mighty kind. Mighty kind,*" Kemper said, reaching to take the plate from the man. But Mr. Ellison would not release it from his grip, instead initiating a sort of stalemate while presenting a mischievous grin.

"*Girls,*" he said, not taking his eyes off Kemper. "Would you like something to eat?"

Caroline and Julie approached cautiously, looking at one another for camaraderie and beginning to nod and say things like *Sure...yeah...uh, sounds great* and *I could eat,* as they left their guard of Bently and began to walk out onto the driveway.

"He okay?" Mr. Ellison asked with a snarky grin. "Doesn't look so good."

"Was up studying most of the night," Kemper added. "Chem final really took it out of him."

"*Hmm*," Mr. Ellison nodded, clearly not taking the bait. "You already in finals? Seems a bit early?" But his entire demeanor changed the minute Caroline and Julie stepped up to the circle and began laying on the charm.

"Oh my gosh. This is *so* nice," Caroline said, totally playing the man with those big brown eyes.

"Actually. *This is so great*," Julie went along. "Our host hasn't offered us the slightest snack or drink."

"*Seriously*?" Kemper responded, clearly finding the comment funny.

"Well, *of course*, young ladies," Mr. Ellison said, now eyeing Kemper like he was one of the boys. He pulled his hand away from the plate in the manner of someone touching something hot, realizing he hadn't let go. "You all enjoy, now. I can come collect the plate later."

"No worries," I told him. "I'll run it up in a bit."

"Great," Mr. Ellison said. "That sounds fine by me." It was amazing the way his entire body language and mood seemed to change the minute the girls began to engage him. "Make sure he gets some," he added as he walked away, pointing toward Bently.

"We will," Caroline said. "Of course we will. Thanks again."

The group watched as the wide-assed man walked back up the sidewalk toward his guests. Laboring with each step, as though a hip might pop loose of its socket or a tendon wave the white flag.

"What a douche," Kemper said.

"I don't know," Julie said. "At least he brought us food."

"*Traitor*," Kemper exclaimed, taking Julie into his arms and sort of dipping her back as they do when a couple takes dance lessons. "*Fraternizing with the enemy.*" She smiled and took a big bite of her bratwurst. "*Vile temptress.*"

Caroline walked over to the boombox on the workbench and began rummaging through a stack of CDs. She selected one out of appreciation for the cover art more than any sort of familiarity with the band and loaded it into the top of the boombox. The cover was mostly baby blue sky with dark mountains outlined in the horizon and a pink road reaching the point of a triangle as it ascended into the distance. Beneath her breath she read the names of songs listed on the back of the case, "*Random Rules...Night Society...Send in the Clouds.*"

"That's a good one," I said. "Send in the Clouds. First one of theirs that got its hooks in me. They grow on you. Though most people think the lead singer can't sing." The opening lyrics were about perfectionism and screwing your way across a foreign land, which made me blush. "Forgot it started that way."

"I like it," she said.

"Yeah. Me too."

"What about this one?" she asked, inviting me closer, moving hair from the nape of her thin neck to reveal beautiful skin. I once read that when an animal is comfortable with you it will lie on its back, exposing its midsection. A show of trust. I moved in place just over her shoulder as she held up an album with an orangish, pinkish moon and a floating teacup beneath a bone-white face with a red clown nose.

"Chill," I said. "Super chill. Died when he was twenty-six."

"Like Cobain."

"No, Cobain was twenty-seven. As were Hendrix, Joplin, and Morrison."

"You're a nerd," she said playfully, as I noticed goosebumps appear upon her skin.

"True story."

"*Guys?*" Trumner said.

A brown Buick LeSabre pulled into the Tarkins' driveway. It was rumored Mrs. Tarkin was trying to get Adam to church for reconciliation when the boy stood upon his bed and defecated. Finley Charles told me and a group of others about it one day in the cafeteria. "Didn't say a word from my understanding, just stood up and dropped a turd." Most of the group laughed due to her use of the word *turd* and others for a lack of knowing how else to respond. I was among the latter. She said her mother learned this from Jenny Bromley, who apparently overheard Mrs. Tarkin speaking with Father Doherty in the vestibule of the church. Yet another verification to me that most adults were merely gossipy little children who simply paid bills and drove us to practice. I felt embarrassed for Adam. Found it unfair that so much of his torment was out in the open like that. But there I stood with the others on an unseasonably warm evening.

Mr. Ellison walked to the edge of the driveway before turning back to his guests and sort of raising his arms like Russell Crowe in that movie where he wore all that badass armor. The one where he was on a mission to enact vengeance upon Joaquin Phoenix for killing his family. I thought it was alright, if not a bit overrated. I much preferred the one about the young woman in nineteenth century China that came out around the same time where they jumped around in trees and ran across rooftops. Me and Trumner went and saw it at the movies after smoking behind Danbury Dollar Cinema and it was pretty epic. Nonetheless, Mr. Ellison really thought he was something. Walking about his guests as though he'd paid for live entertainment.

Moments later, Father Doherty arose from the LeSabre and turned to greet the group across the street. Mr. Ellison nervously walked toward the Genesis I and started cleaning the cooking area with a stainless-steel brush. The rest of the congregation said things such as *Hi, Father...* and...*Good evening...* or *...Surprised to see you here!* along with a number of other disingenuous responses and flat out lies. Same folks who considered themselves good Catholics on Sunday mornings. But Father Doherty paid little attention, instead reaching back inside the LeSabre to retrieve his garments. First pulling a long black robe overhead, followed by what seemed like a little white dress that hung down past his thighs, all the while inaudibly praying beneath his breath. He took great care with the last garment, draping what appeared to be a purple scarf upon the back of his neck where it fell along each side of his body, embroidered at both ends with ancient golden crosses. Mrs. Tarkin appeared at the door, cracking it ever so slightly, as one does when trying to keep an animal from getting out. She seemed small, frail. Far from the woman who used to make us chocolate chip cheeseballs and take us to the video store to rent movies for sleepovers. Not even getting the slightest bit upset when we switched the movie cassette cases out between *The Hunchback of Notre Dame* and that movie where

Denise Richards and Naomi Campbell make out in the pool. Adam told me and Kemper she returned it while we were at school. Only thing she mentioned was that there seemed to be some confusion between what was rented and what was returned. I watched as that same woman opened the door just wide enough for Father Doherty to step inside. The moment he did, the lamp clicked on in Adam's bedroom window. It was in those moments that I started feeling uneasy. Something on a grand scale. And as the rest of the group walked back over to the sofas, talking about the whole ordeal being anticlimactic, I felt an overwhelming urge to leave. Not just Kemper's house or the neighborhood, but to pile into Dufour's Bonneville and get the fuck out of Dodge. Something about the way that light came on in Adam's bedroom, as though he was saying, *WELCOME TO THE SHOW, YOU FUCKS*.

I stood and watched the window for a few moments longer, waiting for something to happen. Most of my view relegated to that of a small swath of ceiling and wall. Such a strange feeling, knowing that Adam was in that same room I'd been in on so many occasions growing up, lying in bed or perhaps down on the carpet where we used to sit shoulder to shoulder paging through old comic books. Adam loved *The Punisher* best, saying, "It wasn't really a choice, you know? Things happened and he was sort of set in motion." He collected everything that was released by Marvel about *The Punisher*, but his favorite were *The Punisher Armory* mags. Adam was so excited to show me those. It was basically Frank Castle, aka The Punisher, as he ran through the weaponry he used on all his missions. Breaking down things such as the standard 9.5-pound weight of an Uzi fully loaded and the difference between a Moeller Viper Knife and a Becker Machax, the former being ideal for carrying, and more specifically, throwing while in combat. Whereas the latter, which it's worth noting, could also be thrown, was more useful in regard to survival/camping. Adam's mind was special in that way. Digesting information, no matter how trivial. "Can't imagine having all those options to take someone out." It all seemed so absurd that some semblance of the boy I used to see as a friend was up there going through some sort of tragic ailment or mental snap. But honestly, I was just frightened. I thought maybe the weed was getting the best of me, verbally telling myself, "Take it easy, man," before casually strolling back into the garage.

Caroline and Julie watched intently as Trumner pulled a yearbook from beneath one of the sofas and broke up a bud. In a matter of minutes, he fashioned a perfectly crafted toothpick-of-a-joint and passed it along to the girls.

"Now, when you roll that, do you want it loose or tight?" Caroline asked.

"Always tight. Otherwise, it'll burn too quickly. Or uneven."

"I hate that."

"Same."

"That Keaton kid in there?" Julie asked, reaching for the yearbook. Trumner pinned the rolling papers between his lips and scraped the stems and seeds from the surface down into his cupped hand. Offered her the yearbook. Every once in a while, Trumner would do something that just came off as smooth, and that was one of those things.

"Nah," Kemper said. "He was still over at Carlisle then."

"Heard he fingered Jenny Kelly," Julie said.

"Half the school's fingered Jenny Kelly. Present company included," Kemper responded, before looking Julie's way and shrugging.

"Not sure how his condition gives him much of an upper hand?" I commented. "More optics than anything."

"Are you shitting me? Dude has catcher's mitts," Trumner said, while making a lude hand gesture that both turned the girls' stomachs and was irrefutably funny as shit.

"*Sick, dude.*"

"Barf."

"Hey, didn't Jenny Kelly go to Notre Dame for a bit?" Kemper asked.

"Yeah, for a quarter or two, but then her dad lost his job," Julie told him. "She was kind of a bitch."

"You're kind of a bitch," Kemper joked.

"I know."

"I broke into her locker and scrawled 'cunt' along the inside of the door," Caroline blurted out.

"Wait, that was you?" Julie asked.

"Practiced Lucida Calligraphy off Word to give it character and distinguish it from my own handwriting. Never told anybody. I'm really stoned."

"You sneaky little bitch," Julie laughed, clearly impressed.

"Show me," I said, while simultaneously standing to locate something to write with. I found a pencil from the workbench that was nubby and nearly worn down to nothing and required added pressure while writing. And found it adorable the way she leaned over the torn piece of carboard, turning her head to the right a bit and biting her lip. Loved the way her thumb and pointer did that thing where the blood ran to the tips because she was pressing so hard. She moved across the cardboard slowly, reminding herself of the attributes that Lucida Calligraphy was to showcase before presenting the sample like a detective showing her findings.

CUNT

"Not how I pictured it."

"No?"

"Guess it sounded more sophisticated when you mentioned it?"

"Perhaps it's the word itself? Some just find it distasteful."

"What size font did you shoot for?"

"Thirty-six, to say...forty-eight?"

"Centered?"

"Of course."

"You two are *super* stoned," Julie declared, and we all lost it.

"You know what we need to play?" Trumner asked, and just like that, they began chanting, "*Futures! Futures! Futures!*" Except for me, as I always found the game to be in bad taste, and the girls, who had no idea what we were talking about. I also had a bit of an aversion to anything that might bring about bad karma.

"The heck's that?" Julie asked, presenting a look of disgust by raising the right side of her lip and furrowing her brow.

"Some shit Bently made up. Sort of entertaining, though mostly childish," Trumner said.

"So how do you play?"

"Flip through the yearbook and close your eyes. Specifically, class photos," Bently told her. "Any will do."

Julie played along, hesitantly raising that pointy nose of hers into the air while flipping blindly through the book. She stopped on Mrs. Kleinfelder's junior class, the enormous head of the teacher consuming nearly all real estate of the square allocated to her identity. There was no denying it, the woman was ugly. Nose, cheeks, and jowls swollen to such a degree that had she not been wearing bifocals, there would be no indication as to where her nose and eyes resided. Just one rotund gaggle of meaty flesh. Perhaps she was smiling. Perhaps she was not, made no matter.

"What's this?" Julie asked.

"Pick one," Bently said, sitting up to where he could see that most of the class was in play. "Any will do."

Michael Stewart was who she named, and I immediately knew the image. Michael was a proper nerd with greasy black hair that wasn't so much combed to the side but rather sculpted in place with the sheen of an oil slick. His cheeks were bulbous and thick as elbows, and there was a scar from some sort of surgery between his nose and top lip. He wore a collared shirt that one might assume was severely wrinkled, though all that could be seen was a few inches below his shoulders.

"Michael chokes to death at a hole-in-the-wall steak house, a mere fifteen minutes after a paramedic finishes his meal and leaves?" Julie said. "I don't get it."

"Well, that's a real shit way to die," Bently explained.

"No honor. Public setting. Probably vomited a little," Trumner played along.

"I mean, I don't understand the game."

"*Okay*," Kemper jumped in. "Go to Bently's."

"You guys are stupid."

"Just do it."

She paged through until she reached Dr. Schrand's freshman class and located Bently's photo. She gave him shit, as he appeared to be wearing the same outfit, which caused Bently to sort of scan his body to ensure that was not the case. She began to smile as she read something absolutely ridiculous.

"Sam Bently is impaled by an elephant while on safari?"

"*See*," Trumner said. "Now that's an honorable way to go."

"How so?" Caroline jumped in.

"I mean, an elephant's fuckin' enormous. There's no shame in being taken out by one of God's most capable beasts."

"Not to mention, highly intelligent," Bently added. "One of the few mammals, besides us, actually capable of grieving. But you're missing the most important part."

"And what's that?"

"*I'm on a fuckin' safari,*" Bently exclaimed. "So, safe to say, I'm filthy rich. Whereas..."

"Whereas," Julie cut him off, hoisting the yearbook with one hand while giving him the signal to stop talking with the other, "Jerry Renner dies while being fisted by Eric Alcott."

"Now you're catching on," Kemper said, sarcastically petting her atop the head.

"Pet me again, and I'll rip your dick off."

"*Hot.*"

"We had this whole other story where Alcott can't get his hand out of Renner's ass and falls down the steps and breaks his neck and eventually dies of positional asphyxiation, but it was just too much to write."

"Classy, guys. Real, classy," I said.

"*Do mine,*" Dufour insisted.

"Already did, screwhead," Bently told him.

"Seriously? When?" Dufour asked, insecurely pulling the yearbook from Julie's lap. "*Fuck's this*? It literally says my head gets screwed off?"

"Yeah, you're a screwhead," Trumner tells him.

"And you're a dick."

"Sometimes."

After which, Trumner playfully jabbed Dufour and Dufour sort of did that thing where he slapped at Trumner's hand. Reminded me of two brothers giving each other shit but trying not to get yelled at by their mom. Kemper straight-armed the back of the couch and looked down to where Julie leaned her head back and gazed into his eyes. Bently was in the midst of that cliché line about getting a room when something caught Kemper's attention.

"Hey, hey..." he said. "Check it out."

He began heading toward the threshold of the door, and the rest of the group followed suit. Julie walked between the tiny crowd and situated herself directly in front of Kemper, leaning back as one might against a tree. Father Doherty was already out the door and nearly to his car as Mrs. Tarkin hurried out after him. He was actively removing the garments he'd put on no more than twenty minutes prior as she unknowingly started to pull and tug at them, as though dressing some sort of overgrown child.

"*Emily, please,*" he said in an attempt to halt her onslaught of desperation. "Now as I said, do try and get some rest and I'll call on you in the morning."

"Wait, you can't go. You can't go now," she said in rapid succession. "*You've seen. You've seen what he is.*"

It was then that Father Doherty grabbed a handful of his robe and pulled it away as to not make contact with the woman. He turned to the group across the street and registered only fear.

The group seemed to freeze. Ellie King stopped midbite on a hotdog and Michael Bohlen removed his ballcap at the bill to satisfy an itch, only to stop before fingernails hit his hair. All stuck in the moment. Unable to move. Father Doherty then became unhinged. "*Get in your homes!*" he said, walking toward them and frantically waving his arms, hoping to direct them inside. "*Each one of you, do as I say! Get inside!*" Then he sort of coughed and brought a hand up to cover his mouth, but something got past, slipping between his fingers and landing in the street with the sound of scattered dice. He looked at the ground in horror before going back to his Buick and shutting himself inside.

"*Wait! Wait! No! No! No!*" Mrs. Tarkin begged, nearly sprawling across the hood as Father Doherty put the Buick in reverse and backed out of the driveway. She collapsed onto the concrete, left weeping and crumpled as he sped away. Such a strange thing to see, a man of the cloth literally fleeing the scene. Father Doherty would later be convicted of sixty-two counts of money laundering for stealing over $380,000 in donations from parishes across the tri-state area to fund his sumptuous lifestyle. So, perhaps it was this compromise in faith that made him no match for the goings-on in the Tarkin home? Regardless, his true character had been witnessed by many and remembered by some.

After a few moments, David Steimle and his wife, Maureen, walked over and crouched down to comfort Mrs. Tarkin, slowly helping her up and into the house. But they refused to go inside. She begged them to come in, but instead they sort of looked past the threshold as though a dark cave that might contain a bear or at the very least, bats. Edward Kreimbourgh walked to the middle of the street and crouched down to investigate. Without turning back to the group, he hollered over his shoulder, *"It's teeth. We've got teeth."*

"Well, that was awful," Julie said.

"What was he so afraid of?" Caroline asked.

"More than afraid," Trumner added. "Terrified."

The rest of the group watched the Steimle's forcibly close Mrs. Tarkin inside the house, Mr. Steimle actually going so far as to hold the front door shut while Mrs. Steimle muttered words of affirmation through the long column window alongside the door. But I focused solely on Adam's window above. Mr. Ellison stood at the edge of his driveway, sort of walking the property line, unable to commit to the heightened drama taking place across the street. Mrs. Tarkin desperately pleaded on the other side of the door as the light in Adam's window clicked off.

"And this concludes our irregularly scheduled program," Bently announced.

"Okay, Julie, my darling, now that you've caught on, it's your turn," Kemper said, walking the girl back toward the sofa with an arm around her shoulder. "Step one...grab a beer..." which he assisted with by grabbing a beer from the cooler and cracking the tab with a *THWAK*. "Step two...sit your lil ass right here on the sofa. And step three...close your eyes, turn the page, and blindly create destruction with the point of a finger."

Julie followed instructions as the rest of the group gathered around to see whose fate would be left in her hands. She brought a pointer down near the center of the page on Mr. Rusk's class and opened her eyes. "Rachel McNeily," she announced.

"Poor Rachel," Trumner said. "She never had a chance."

Rachel was thin and sickly looking, likely an easy mark to wipe from the planet, with green alternative streaks in her hair and a tongue ring she displayed by slightly opening her mouth. She once stopped talking for nearly a week, communicating only by marking different body parts with messages to her parents, teachers, and classmates. Found it kind of funny, really, and sort of clever how she scrawled *don't* upon one eyelid and *care* on the other, proffering the message by simply closing her eyes. She also etched *FUCK OFF!* on her nail beds and happily brought them together when Mrs. Balkin asked her to read aloud.

"*Fuck her up, Jules,*" Dufour said.

"My mom calls me Jules."

"How sweet," Kemper said. "Now, what you got?"

I remained focused upon Adam Tarkin's bedroom window. With the tiny, sloped roof just outside, running parallel to the front of the house. When younger, me, Tarkin, and Kemper used to bring our sleeping bags out on that roof and lie on our backs, looking up at the stars. Tarkin knew a shit ton about the solar system and told us random facts, like how one day on Venus was equivalent to a whole year on Earth due to the slow rotation of the planet. Or how Saturn's rings were composed of ice and rock, and how the planet is so dense that it could actually float in a tub of water had you a big enough tub. And how

Uranus is the only planet to rotate on its side at a tilt of roughly ninety degrees. Which of course elicited Kemper and I to go into a litany of euphemisms in regard to our assholes, classmates' assholes, and each other's moms' assholes.

"You good?" Caroline asked.

"Huh?" I responded. "Yeah. Yeah. Fine."

"I'm sure he'll be okay."

"Hope so."

I could feel her gaze, though I was unable to pull my eyes from Adam's window, waiting for some indication that he was still inside. Sitting in that dark little room. Or, perhaps even looking out? Judging all of us. Reversing the show and seeing how pitiful we all were. How sad. And maybe he was cussing us? Or casting out some sort of curse or justified prayer? All I know is I was feeling pretty lousy.

"What do ya say we go for a walk?" Caroline asked, but that was not what pulled my attention. Instead, it was when I suddenly found her soft little hand in mine. Fingers casually intertwined with my own. She pulled me forward, and I playfully anchored in place so that my torso leaned out past my feet until I was finally forced to take a step. "That's the spirit," she told me. "Hey, we're gonna take a little walk. Be back in a few."

"Yeah. Yeah," Julie said, dismissing us with a fluttery wave, keeping her focus on the yearbook where she'd already begun to map out Rachel McNeily's fate. There was mention of leprosy and months of decay in a secluded farmhouse where she'd suffer death and eventually coagulate and seep through the floorboards, but Caroline and I were long since down the driveway and walking away from the house by that point.

"Here," I said, providing a gentle tug and directing our path away from the sidewalk. "Let's cut through the Bartletts'. Avoid the adults."

"No argument there."

Between the Bartletts' and a neighboring fence was a section of maybe fifty yards letting out onto Stover Road. Stover led all the way to the back of the neighborhood where the older houses were first built. Trees lined the road, giving the area an inviting sort of privacy. Across the street, Mr. Graber walked his Siberian husky, Bascombe, and spoke beneath his breath. The dog looked our way, presenting its striking blue eyes and graceful build. Mr. Graber was known to talk through projects aloud as he walked, and most neighbors thought him to be a bit eccentric, but to me it sort of made sense. Whenever I was trying to figure something out, or at least a path forward, the idea always seemed to come to me while on a walk. It was while walking that I weighed the pros and cons of playing soccer for Coach Pullman. *Ah, no. You're miserable and the man's a fuckin' dick.* And it was walking that brought me the topic for my term paper on orphan diseases and insufficient federal funding. *Regardless of your political beliefs, the Obama administration was a huge advocate for research and clinical trials for diseases affecting populations of two hundred thousand individuals or less.* And it was while walking, during those very moments, that I thought I might be falling in love with Caroline Jehn. *Not that we can't take it slow, of course we can, we literally just met. But there's something here, right? Something very real.*

The Lendermans' steepled roof seemed to impale the sun, as though the sharp slant of roof said, *Hey, hey, hey, where do you think you're going?* in an attempt to stave off the night. But moments later, night was upon us, and houselights began to switch on either manually or by way of timers. We let go of each other's hands but still walked close enough to occasionally brush against one another as we sauntered down the street. Caroline started walking ahead of me, backward, making blatant eye contact and demanding that I show her my house.

"Oh, I don't know. Our house was the first one built. Nothing special. Where do you live?"

"You know where Crowley and Sutton intersect?"

"I do," I responded, unknowingly registering a bit of surprise.

"*Ohhh, I caught you!*" Caroline said, pointing at me and laughing. I paused in my tracks, unsure of what she saw. And honestly, she wasn't wrong. Being friends with Julie Derringer made me assume she'd lived in Ivy Hills, by the swim club, or at least Coldstream. Inadvertently assuming that she'd come from wealth. But she would continue to exceed my expectations.

"*No. Wait. What?*"

"You're a bad liar."

"What's happening?"

"You have no game face. *What?* You shocked that a girl who attends Mt. Notre Dame Academy lives in Lower Guild?"

"Hey, I like Lower Guild, okay? Don't peg me for a snob. My grandma and I used to go down there to get soft serve from The Grocery Bag all the time."

"*Yeah, yeah.*"

"You do sort of surprise me, though."

"Why's that?"

"I don't know. I guess most kids our age are pretty easy to peg...You, I can't quite figure out."

"Oh, yeah?"

"Yeah."

"Okay, tell me about it. Start with Trumner."

"Trumner? Oh, he's pretty harmless, really. Good attention. Bad attention. Both are acceptable. And there aren't really any limitations as far as what you can say to him, which I've always enjoyed because I'm the type who constantly plays things over and over in my head. Afraid I might have offended someone. Beating myself up. And with Trumner, that's never much of a concern. It's like he has his own sort of Iron Dome. Nothing really touches him."

"Interesting."

"He is."

"I meant you. But yes, that's also fair. Okay, Julie. Thoughts on Julie."

"Pointy. Sharp. Piercing. Features and personality. Snobbery and bitchiness for days, but that's also kind of the draw, right? Can cut a bitch down during the proper circumstances. But build her up by highlighting good qualities. Always dressed to the hilt. Not so much based on look but brand. And her mom's a heroically fierce lawyer that she both idolizes and secretly despises."

"That's true. Holy shit, that's all so spot on."

"And you? Well, I guess that's sort of a *to be continued* type deal."

She smiled wide and those big, beautiful eyes worked over me. It made me realize that there was beauty, personal to your own desires, that could absolutely end you, spend you, and leave you speechless. Nothing was said for a bit, just eye contact and energy that you could almost see.

"We used my aunt's address," she said.

"What?"

"So, I could go to Notre Dame. She lives up near Prevalent Park. That white house with the shrubs shaped like animals."

"I know that house," I said, once again failing to present an acceptable game face.

"She's not weird. Just bored."

"I never said she was weird."

"We're not close or anything, but she's alright. She comes to some of my volleyball games. But she's always crocheting. You know what that is?"

"Wait. At your games?"

"Yeah. She doesn't seem to be self-aware. *Holy shit, maybe she is weird?*"

We began laughing at the absurdity of the thought.

"So, she'll be sitting in the bleachers like makin' a blanket or something?"

"Among other things."

"Just workin' on a pair of mittens while some crazy rally is goin' on?"

"*That's exactly right.* Oh, my God. She was actually sewing mittens one game and showin' me them after. Like right after the *good game* procession," she told me, grabbing my bicep and laughing her ass off. "*Okay, she is weird. She's really fuckin' weird.*"

"But weird is good."

"Agreed. Weird is good."

We stopped in front of a house with the family room window wide open to the street. Venetian blinds pulled up though slightly drooping on one side, causing the view of the family sitting inside, watching television, to come off a bit cattywampus. The mother and daughter were snuggled beneath a blanket so that the only thing that could be seen were their faces and little knuckles coming up and pulling the blanket snuggly beneath their chins. And the father sat with an arm around the back of the couch, his son sitting beneath with his knees up and socked feet upon the cushion. The way the television screen played against them gave off the impression of fish displayed in an aquarium.

"What do you think they're watching?" Caroline asked.

"Dunno? Probably some Disney movie, given their ages. Maybe Nickelodeon?"

"Oh, come on. You can do better than that," she challenged. "Make them more interesting. Surprise me."

"Um," I thought, catching on that she was playing a game similar to *Futures! Futures! Futures!* but instead, it was our game. Just the two of us. "*Beastmaster.*"

She snickered and scrunched her nose. "What's that?"

"Oh, it's awful and wonderful and old as shit. My dad made me watch it all the time when I was little. Can't remember too much other than the main character has these two ferrets, Kodo and Podo, that he carries in his pouch and sends off to retrieve keys and stuff. And there are these monsters that trap people in their batlike wings, encasing and sort of digesting them. Scared the shit out of me. They open those wings, and skulls and bones drop onto the ground. It's wild."

"Sounds wholesome."

"Absolutely," I said, nodding and smiling. "My dad and I used to have these nights he referred to as parties where we'd raid the pantry for cookies and chips and candy. Anything was fair game. I remember him showing me all his favorite movies, and most of them were pretty good, honestly. You know there's an actual movie called *Octopussy?*"

"I was not aware."

"James Bond. Not sure which number or anything, but the cover has him standing in his regular suave, tuxedoed look with a woman behind him and a bunch of slim female arms coming around his body like an octopus. Pretty clever."

"Sounds riveting."

"Oh, come on. What does your dad watch?" I asked, laughing.

"Nothing," she said. I noted the energy shift. Something heavy. "Not anymore. He passed away a few years ago."

"Oh, I'm so sorry. I didn't mean to..."

"*Oh, stop. It's fine.* I mean, definitely far from ideal, but what can you do, right?"

"What was it?"

"Cancer."

"*God*. I feel like it's always cancer."

"Yeah. It wasn't quick. That's the part that hurt, seeing him in pain. Day after day. This man who was so lively. Always joking and messing around. He was highly immature but so sincere. We'd sit and talk for hours, and shit, I was only twelve when he died. But he'd come in and lie across the bottom of my bed when he got home from work and we'd run through everything. And he genuinely wanted to know. Was interested in my day. What was going on with me. That's what pisses me off the most. I mean, if we could talk like that when I was twelve, what could we talk about now? Or when I'm twenty, or forty? He was just a cool guy. And I guess the older I get, the more I realize we need more *cool guys* in the world, or something? I don't know?"

"Sounds right," I said.

"Wanna cheer me up?"

"Of course. Anything."

"Show me your house."

I unknowingly began to walk in the direction of my house, explaining the nuances of our household. "We can. We absolutely can, but no interaction. Zero. Don't want my parents staring at me and saying things like, '*Are you on pot?*'"

"*Shut up*! *They do not say that*!?"

"Oh, but they do. You're talking about people who haven't so much as sniffed alcohol. Kemper once left a roach on the table on our back patio and my dad went to knock it off and step on it thinking it was a moth, and my mom was all, '*Wait! It's a doobie!*'"

"*She called it a doobie?*" Caroline said, belly laughing.

"She really did. Ended up being an interrogation, which promptly spread from my house to Kemper's and ended at Trumner's, where he fell on the sword."

"Team player."

"Oh, for sure. Dude's a saint with stuff like that."

"I don't really have any friends like that."

"Really? What about Julie?"

"Eh, she's sort of a flake. I'm sure at some point she'll ditch me and start hanging with Erin Schaffer or Molly Donavan. There's a pattern with her that causes her to move on. Not sure if people eventually see through her or what? I mean, she's alright. Can be funny and all, just not sure there's a lot of depth there or anything."

"I get it. I've never really been a guy's guy. I mean, I love those dudes, but I'm not sure I always fit. And I get worn out. Quiet, I guess. Need to charge my battery."

"By watching *Beastman*!"

"*Master*. But yes, by watching *Beastmaster*."

My house sat at the end of Stover Road and always felt a bit of an outcast from the rest of the neighborhood. As though the rest of the houses in the neighborhood had deemed it unworthy or it was assembled by a completely different builder. And it wouldn't have been one of the prettier houses had a census poll been taken. The upkeep of the grass and shrubbery was less than adequate, if not flat out neglectful. And the siding was moss-worn where two pine trees consistently tickled the house when provided motivation by the slightest breeze. The windows were also in desperate need of replacing, trapping moisture between the panes so that much of them seemed fogged over. But the main window looking into the family room and kitchen was crystal clear. Inside my dad sliced portions of what may or may not have been chicken as my mom poured a glass of milk. Both of which were delivered to a small television tray sitting in front of one of those automatic recliners that rose up to help those who struggled to stand. And then there was Grandma Dar, standing in front of the window with her tiny little hunchback overshadowing her tiny, folded shoulders and one little arthritic hand coming up to shield her view like a visor so she could look out the window.

"My grandma lives with us. Or, should I say, we kind of live with her. We moved in after my grandpa passed, to help out. Honestly, can't remember not having her around."

"She's tiny."

"Oh, small as shit. Pretty sure she's shrinking. She actually used to be a decent-sized lady. Not big or anything, but strong. I only know that from pictures. She's got rheumatoid arthritis now. Her poor little fingers are all folded up. She was still writing checks up until a few years ago. It was kind of fascinating watching her pay the bills when I was little. But she's pretty out of it now. Was sharp up until this summer, then all of a sudden her mind just seemed to drop off. She used to tell me wild stories. Her family used to own a farm."

"You mean, your family?"

"Yeah, I guess."

Grandma Dar grew up in what could only be viewed as intergenerational wealth. Her father followed the practices of his father before him and passed it down. She spent most of her days after school as a crop scout. Said each afternoon she'd come home and hang up her skirt and blouse to meet her mother's expectations, before heading out to the orchard. As was her routine, she'd first count buds, blooms, and fruitlets to best get an idea of thinning for better fruit size and profit. While doing so, she'd also look for velvety brown or greenish spots on the undersides of leaves to identify apple scabs. Taking note of cutworm larvae or fire blight. Determining what could be salvaged. And then would come her favorite part, collecting insects by using a sweep net. Swinging the net from side to side in one-hundred-eighty-degree arcs with the lower edge of the net slightly ahead of the upper to catch insects as they fell from the leaves. She would then shake them out of the net onto a white beat cloth. Most stood out and were not hard to spot, but insects such as the southern corn beetles were harder to notice on account of coloration. She enjoyed watching them intermingle, "Like witnessing an entire city from above," she told me. I spent a good deal of time out in the garden with her, asking about the different bugs and plants and imagined I was on a farm. It seemed like such an ancient and magical way to live.

"She's cute," Caroline said.

"Yeah. She's a good one. Tough upbringing, but you'd never know it."

"Like what?"

"Not sure of the details, really. My mom just always said that. She wasn't able to have kids of her own, so they adopted my mom when she was two or three." I didn't go into the things Grandma Dar and my mom discussed in the family room after they thought I'd fallen asleep. Not because I was embarrassed or anything, but more on account of what Caroline shared about losing her dad. I didn't want to get caught up in the sadness. "Anyway, there you have it. My sins have been washed clean."

"*Uh, not so fast.* I think you need to sneak inside and grab us a snack."

"Are you shitting me?" There was a pantry just inside the garage door leading into the house where my mom kept excess supplies and groceries, but not likely anything that would constitute an actual snack. It was more canned goods and pasta boxes, that sort of thing, but my wheels were already spinning.

"I want to watch through the window and see if your parents ask if you've been *doing pot*."

"Not happening," I said, feeling a rush of relief as she began laughing and wrapped an arm around mine.

"*Robert Bausch, are you on pot?*" she said in a parental tone, leaning into me. Pressing her body against my arm. A moment that would never truly leave me. A core memory. So imbedded within my brain that it was impossible to pry any portion of it away.

As clear a memory as I would ever have.

PITFALL!

It wasn't so much a search party as a gathering of curiosity. Caroline and I wouldn't find out until we reached the top of Spinning Wheel Drive as to what had taken place at the Tarkins' while we were away. Trumner came pounding up the sidewalk with Dufour in tow. Pounding would be the proper descriptive, what with the boy's loafing, sloppy strides and the way his size twelve sneakers pattered off the sidewalk with overwhelming weight and substantial force. A few of the parents walked through backyards with flashlights, dispassionately calling Adam's name, but none of them seemed to be invested. Their hearts just weren't in it. Which was fine on account of Trumner's complete investment in the events, details, and unknowns. And perhaps the adults should not have been faulted too stringently, as none other than Alan

Bremer claimed to have witnessed anything. And what he saw was merely what may or may not have been the boy, Adam Tarkin, out of the corner of his eye while stepping away from the group to have a smoke.

But Trumner had seen it all. Watched as Adam's mom walked down the front hallway of the house, flipping off lights in her wake, watched as her shadow ascended the steps, until a light was struck like a match at the top, where she miraculously appeared out of the darkness. Pausing, momentarily, before stepping into Adam's room. Likely saying a prayer or gaining her wits with a few slow, deep breaths.

"Guys, it was fuckin' *epic!* Tarkin's mom was up in his room, and the lights were out and then *BOOM*, there was this bright light on her, and she was shieldin' her eyes and shit." While saying that last part he did a sort of reenactment by bringing his palms up to block an imaginary bright light. But I knew immediately what it was. "Next thing, the light pops off and Tarkin comes crawling out his bedroom window, scuddles across the roof, and drops down into the grass on the side of the house." He noted there was a sound similar to when someone gets the wind knocked from them. "None of the adults up there even heard it, but I caught it all. Shit's better than television."

Kemper and Julie sauntered up behind the group, casual and cool. Kemper with an arm draped around her neck where his wrist limply hung off her shoulder. Julie obnoxiously chomping on gum that she proceeded to pop within the beak of her mouth, making that all too familiar snapping sound.

"*Kemper,*" I asked. "What happened?"

"Not sure, man. I'm pretty lit. Whatever Trumner's reporting. Give or take."

"Give or take? What's that supposed to mean?" Trumner asked.

"*Kemper?*"

"Seriously, Bauschy. *I don't know,* okay? He got loose is all."

"You're talkin' about him like he's a dog or somethin'," Julie said, eliciting laughter, which caused Kemper to nod, wasted and unable to speak, mouthing *I was...I really was.* Doing that widemouthed laughter that occurs when someone finds something so funny they can't catch their breath to get the words out.

"It's not funny. He could be in trouble. *We* could be in trouble."

"Oh, come on, man. Tarkin's lost it, but he's not dangerous, man."

"Mrs. Cummings might disagree," I said. *"And could you quit doing that?"* Julie snapped one last pop of gum before realizing the request was being sent her way. She then raised her eyebrows in a slightly shocked and annoyed fashion.

"Dude, relax. Look, Tarkin's fine, man. He'll turn up."

"Yeah," Trumner said. "He might gnaw on a neighbor's dog or somethin', but he'll resurface."

I put a middle finger a mere two inches from Trumner's face without looking his way, keeping my focus on Kemper. Dufour mimicked the action of eating what he wanted the group to believe was a small dog. Perhaps a Shih Tzu or Pomeranian. Rotating the imaginary beast in the manner of a piece of corn. Trumner leaned in and kissed my finger, causing me to lower my hand and wipe it clean on my jeans. Caroline was the only other one taking the moment seriously, more on account of my being upset than any overwhelming concern.

"Look," Kemper said. "The adults are on the hunt, and the girls are leaving at eleven. And I'm sure Trumner's mommy will be picking him up soon."

"I'm crashing on the couch, dickhead. I told you that already," Trumner said, before quietly mumbling beneath his breath, displaying a rare semblance of embarrassment, "And I can drive myself. Just need an adult in the car is all."

"My point is," Kemper said, "can't we just enjoy what little night we have left?"

"Yes," Dufour said. "I vote yes."

"I second that motion," Trumner said. "The motion for fun." Saying this last part and pointing at Kemper, who pointed back and nodded his head enthusiastically.

"*That's it*," Kemper said. "That's the spirit. That's what I'm talkin' about." Kemper closed in on me, playfully bringing me into a headlock-type hug. "Come on, Bauschy. You know you wanna. *Come on.*"

"*Okay, fine*," I conceded, raising my palms in surrender. "Fine. Whatever."

Subsequently, I would go on to tell Julie to stop snapping her gum three more times before we returned to the garage. Most of the group had lost interest in Tarkin by then, though Trumner was still saying things like "*Damndest thing I've ever saw*" and "*Fuckin' epic*" while rolling another joint. Caroline pointed out that he might have that condition where once completing an activity, he must immediately begin again from scratch. Only, his particular activity was getting us stoned as shit. Kemper agreed she was onto something as he placed a shot of Jager in front of Trumner and shortly thereafter Bently and Dufour.

"Ladies, something with a little more meat to it?" he said, holding up the bottle while passively cupping his crotch.

"Subtle, douche. Subtle," Julie teased.

The adults seemed just as uninterested as the teenagers by that point, returning to a small firepit where Mr. Ellison manipulated embers and logs with a metal fire poker. I doubted he even left the driveway. While the others were out searching for Tarkin, bet that fat sonofabitch mumbled shit like *"It's never a good idea to leave a fire unattended"* or *"One of us should hang back, you know, in case he turns up."* In the front window of the Tarkins' house, the Steimle's were once again playing the role of the good Samaritans, Mrs. Steimle going so far as to drape a blanket over Mrs. Tarkin's shoulders as though a recently rescued refugee or somethin'. The same people who wouldn't step foot in that house an hour earlier were first responders now that Adam had vacated the premises. Real heroes. Type who show up once the flames are extinguished.

An officer pulled into the Tarkins' driveway, causing Trumner and the rest of our group to giggle with excitement. That heightened excitement that goes along with breaking the law on a minor offense as, well, a minor. Which led to him and Dufour singing that Judas Priest song that simply stated that phrase over and over again, about breaking the law. Which Caroline and I found extremely obnoxious and caused Kemper to head over to the garage door opener on the wall and punch the glowing button.

"Let's lower visibility a bit," he said, sucking from a joint wedged in the corner of his mouth, monitoring the descending door and pausing it strategically at knee level. He then spun the threaded wheel of his lighter and brought a few candles to light before placing one on the coffee table and another on the workbench along the far wall.

"Lovely fragrance," Bently said.

"Don't be a jackass. They're my mom's."

"Dude, that shit's gonna have me sneezing my balls off," Trumner complained.

"You'll survive, princess. Promise."

"RoseSmatter?" Julie asked. "My mom buys that sometimes too. My favorite. Are you trying to seduce me?"

"I am. I truly am. My entire existence revolves around getting in your good graces."

"And pants," Bently followed.

Caroline immediately went on into rubbing her eyes and clearing her throat before Kemper offered to grab her a glass of water. I followed him inside and leaned against the kitchen counter as the icemaker struggled to regurgitate a few cubes of ice. He knew what I was gonna say before I even opened my mouth. Knew my heart was always at the forefront of my decisions. To this day, I'm not sure if that's a good or bad thing. But I guess I'd like to believe good.

"Don't start, Bauschy. I feel for Tarkin too, man, but what are we supposed to do?"

"Maybe just go have a look? I don't know. Check in with Mrs. Tarkin?"

"No can do, brother. I'm ripped. You're ripped. We're all ripped."

"I'm not that ripped."

"Dude, look in the mirror," he told me. "Seriously, pop on into the bathroom and have a gander, because your eyes are red as a baboon's asshole."

"I don't know, man. I guess it all makes me feel like shit. I mean, he used to be our friend, right? That should count for something. There's history there."

"Most of which I'd honestly prefer to forget. No offense. We had some good times, but man, there was some crazy shit."

And I knew exactly what he was referring to.

It was the summer leading up to fifth grade. Me and Kemper were sitting on the front porch of Tarkin's house. The porch was long and ran parallel to the front of the house. We had just finished *jumping the hedge*, as we liked to call it. The whole idea was to run the length of the porch before launching into the air and jumping the sloppy, overgrown hedges, which was no simple feat at that point in our lives. Kemper was the best, usually bringing his knees up, heels together like a skateboarder on a half-pipe, but me and Tarkin struggled. Me, consistently grazing the top of the hedges with the bottom of my sneakers, causing branches to bob in my wake. And Tarkin, well, he may as well have dived directly into the damned things. Always leaving a substantial amount of destruction in his path. *"Lordy, Tarkin. Looks like a gotdamned tornado ripped through."*

Afterwhile, Kemper and I found ourselves sitting in Mr. and Mrs. Tarkin's rockers while Tarkin went to fetch us some popsicles from the freezer. I was talking about that part in *Predator* where Jesse *'The Body'* Ventura goes all hog wild with that M134 Minigun, and how cool it was when the ammo ran out, and those barrels rotated with a hum. "Just badass, man. Can't imagine firing that thing, ya know?" But Kemper's attention was elsewhere. Subtle at first. A kind of tiny leak that seemed to spread across the ceiling of the porch just outside the front door. Only, it seemed to be widening and receding. Which reminded me of that game Pitfall! on the video game console my dad got me the previous Christmas with one hundred and fifty different games to choose from. This was the one with those pixilated swamps that shrank and grew, expanding and contracting like lungs, as the player had to time the jump just right by grabbing a vine to make it across. The vine swinging back and forth like a pendulum. The graphics were toast, but my dad loved it when *he* was a kid and I had to admit, it was pretty fun. Each level got a bit more challenging until alligators eventually started coming out of the swamp to feed on your player. Anyway, that's what I was reminded of when the first droplet smattered upon the cement porch.

"Fuck's that?" Kemper asked, as the two of us stood and walked over for a closer look.

Kemper crouched down to investigate and I said, which I now realize was sort of moronic, "Don't touch it."

"Well, no shit."

Then came another droplet. And another. In rapid succession. The last striking the fabric of Kemper's white t-shirt.

"For shit's sakes," he said, standing quickly and causing us both to sort of panic and hop over some bushes and out onto the front lawn. It was then that we realized the pond above had spread nearly five feet across the porch ceiling and roughly three feet wide. No longer pulsing, but rather a tiny island dripping what looked to be bright red blood and a litany of other junk. "Looks like cracked eggs or somethin'."

"That's not normal," I added.

Shortly after, Tarkin stepped out onto the front porch with a popsicle in each hand and another embedded within the butthole of his mouth. He immediately handed the popsicles off and mumbled something about how his dad was *gonna be pissed* before popping open the front door and saying, "*Dad, it's happening again!*" His dad's footsteps echoed off the walls of the empty hallway. At one point there had been a number of family pictures on those walls, but they'd been removed in the weeks prior. "My dad thinks a litter of baby racoons, or something keep getting trapped up there and can't figure their way out. Happened a few times now." But when Tarkin's dad stepped out onto the front porch, the look on his face registered another story. As though he were witnessing the return of some sort of ancient act of violence that only he was capable of seeing. Tarkin's dad was thin, gaunt, with veins that began to show through translucent skin. Some claimed him wrought with cancer. Others said he'd been taken by addiction. But no one knew for sure what was taking place within the walls of that house.

"Boys, go on and find somethin' to do," he said, never taking his eyes from the ceiling. By the time we were down the street, he had already screwed the faucet loose on the side of the house and began spraying down the ceiling and substances upon the porch.

"It's really pissin' him off," Tarkin said. "Can't figure out how they're gettin' in there."

"Dude, there's not much we can do for him at the moment," Kemper said, handing me Caroline's glass of water. "Besides, we've got two goodlooking girls out in the garage that seem to have taken a liking to us, and I, for one, don't intend to blow it."

Just then, the garage door popped open with that suction sound that accompanies external doors lined with weatherstripping. Julie peeked her pointy little nose in and begged entrance. Kemper made it playfully clear that his parents didn't want anyone in the house while they were away, especially teenage girls, but both Kemper and Julie were destined to defy that request.

"*Julie Eileen Derringer*," Kemper began, with an overzealous pointing finger, "you know *full well* that there are no females allowed in the Kemper household without parental supervision! *Now take off all your clothes!*"

She stepped her socked feet into the front room and began to slowly raise her t-shirt up over her thin abdomen, grabbing at the bottom fabric with opposite hands, like they do in pornos. Both Kemper and I would be lying if we denied being aroused, but just as quickly she let loose of her shirt, allowing it to fall back down below her waistline, and raised two middle fingers.

"I need to use the phone," she said. "And my middle name isn't Eileen."

An enormously flirtatious smile stretched the perimeter of Kemper's face, which made him look a little mad to me. Not mad as in angry or frustrated, but more along the lines of slightly drunken or unhinged. Similar to the actor in that movie hobbling through the hotel with an axe trying to kill his wife and son. Without changing expression, he pointed to a cordless phone on its cradle in the front room, where Julie went into the darkness and began punching numbers and speaking to one of her parents.

"You're slightly pathetic," I said. "You know that?"

"We're all slightly to mostly pathetic."

"Do you even like her?"

"Does she even like me?" he followed, walking toward me and wrapping an arm around my neck in brotherly solidarity. "The answer is that she does, at least for tonight. And I do, at least for tonight. And tonight, my brother, is all we've got."

"You're a creep. Likeable, I'll give you that, but still a little on the creepy side."

"*True story.*"

The two of us laughed. From the darkness of the front room, we heard a beep and Julie fumbling to return the phone to its cradle.

"*Good news,*" she said. "My mom's letting us hang until midnight."

"That *is* good news," Kemper said, pulling me close in another headlock-type embrace. "*That most certainly is good news.*"

"You're so annoying," I giggled.

"Should I leave you two alone?" Julie asked, before immediately going into a defensive stance as Kemper let loose of me and scooped her up fireman-style over a chiseled shoulder. I pulled back the garage door and ushered them outside. Stephen Malkmus' guitar began to work through the progressions of *Night Society* as I closed the door and muffled all sound. I stepped into the darkness of the front room and took in the near silence for a few minutes, needing a minute away from the madness of my friends. Guilt blanketed me as I walked over to have a look through the front blinds. Then a swath of light severed the room, and Caroline's silhouette stepped up into the doorway.

"You comin' back out?" she asked as she closed the door behind her.

"Yeah, just getting a little reset."

"From me?" she said, feigning offense. "No. Of course not."

She walked up and peered out the blinds alongside me, eliciting that metallic sound when she hooked a finger and bent them down.

"You know what I feel worse about?"

"What?"

"I feel like I abandoned him. Because I got scared. The day before he went to the hospital, there was an incident on the bus. Bunch of kids started distancing themselves after that. And I guess I was kind of one of them."

"What happened?"

"It's stupid, really. And honestly probably just symptomatic of what he was dealing with. But that day he walked up the aisle of the bus and sat in the seat with Kemper and I just as he always had. Only, there didn't seem much life to him. I remember Kemper saying, '*Damn Tarkin*, you need to get more sleep,' or some shit. And he did, he looked almost zombified. After that, we weren't really paying attention. Not until we heard a bunch of kids making a fuss and the sound of something rolling down the aisle and under the seats."

Mae Greenburgh was the first I heard. She called out with an unequivocal scream and immediately started smacking at bugs that very clearly traipsed across her clothing and up into her hair. And then the entire bus was in a sort of frenzy, doing much the same. Somehow there was an instant sort of infestation of buzzing and crawling insects. "Kemper and I were completely thrown by it all. Simply watching the madness from the back of the bus. That's when we noticed Tarkin. He was sitting by the window eating an apple that was rotten as hell. Maggots and fruit flies moving beneath the thin skin of the fruit. In his teeth." His backpack sat in his lap completely unzipped on each side, so much so that the front of the bag dropped open like a trapdoor. There were a few apples and peaches still housed in the pouch of the backpack, but the rest had spilled out and rolled down beneath the seats and into the aisle when the bus went down The Cut in the Hill. "It was absolute chaos. And he seemed completely unaware. That apple turning to mush in his mouth. Insects climbing back behind his ears. I remember that so vividly. It's weird."

"Holy shit."

"Yeah. After that, I guess Kemper and I didn't really know how to navigate the situation, ya know?"

"I mean, you were only in what? Fifth grade?"

"Somethin' like that. Still feel like a piece of shit."

It was less than half an hour later that the lights went kaputt. Julie was sitting in Kemper's lap on one of the two sofas at that point, openly providing him all the attention her bony little frame could offer. They spoke in hushed tones and leaned into each other. The music switched back to Radiohead. This time, *The Bends*, leading Trumner and Bently into an open debate as to whether or not it or *OK Computer* was their best album. Bently was literally in the middle of saying, "Well, you know where I stand," when the lights went off with a click. We could feel the energy of the *whole* house, hell, the *whole* neighborhood die. Caroline jumped, not knowing how to respond, and Kemper spouted off in the darkness about the likelihood of a car having struck that pole down off Munich Drive. Which led him into an unwarranted and strange parental-sounding tirade about folks driving too fast down that road and the city's irresponsible location knowing that the corner was a bit of a hazard.

"Thanks for your input, *Dad*," Trumner said. "At least these stinky candles were pre-lit and ready to roll."

Kemper raised a middle finger without removing his gaze from Julie as I pulled the emergency release cord of the garage door. At first it began to lower, but I wielded an arm back in the fashion of a little kid making a muscle and slowly guided the door up its tracks. The other garage door remained closed to block the group and allow them to openly smoke and drink, but I opened the other wide. As quickly as the door clicked into place at the top of the track, Dave Ayres stepped inside the garage. Trumner brought a lit joint behind his back before noting that his other hand contained a can of Coors Original, which he then nonchalantly brought behind his back as well. Dave was tall and handsome, at least from what the teenage girls' and moms in the neighborhood's comments and whispers implied each time he came around. He never married or had kids, which gave him sort of a strange appeal. The men saw him as the consummate bachelor, free to do as he pleased, and the women saw him as a fantasy figure that might walk into their homes and ravage them while their husbands were away.

"Easy," he said to Dufour, who began collecting cans and roaches from a little tin ashtray. "Not here to come down on you, just wanted to make sure you all are good."

I couldn't help myself, asking, "Did they find him?"

Dave brought a strong ringed hand to his mouth and covered it before shaking his head that they hadn't. It seemed to be a state championship ring, though none of us knew for what sport or achievement it might have been awarded. "Officer did a couple of spins around the block with the ole spotlight but didn't seem to see anything. He hit his lights and left when the power went out. Probably that pole down on Munich by the front entrance."

"*See*," Kemper said. "Told you."

"*You're a dork*," Trumner said playfully.

"Anyway, if you all need anything, just pop up and grab us, okay?"

"We will," Julie said, before Kemper reached up and closed her open mouth, causing her to smack him playfully in the chest.

As he walked away I began blindly rummaging through the workbench, knocking over a can of WD-40 and spray paint. Moments later I located what I was looking for and clicked the oval rubber button upon the long handle of a flashlight. The kind that cops often carried in case they needed a readily accessible weapon.

"I'm gonna take a walk around the neighborhood really quick, see if I see anything."

"Good Lord, Bauschy, he'll turn up eventually. I mean, how far's he gonna get?" Kemper said.

"I'll go," Caroline said.

"Shit," Trumner said. "I could take a walk. Better than sitting our asses in here for the next hour watching old suckface and fuckface snuggle."

"Yeah, okay," Bently agreed. "We'll just leave the little lovebirds alone for a while."

With that, Dufour loaded up a backpack with cans of PBR and was praised by the rest of us for his ingenuity during such a dark hour, which Bently declared overdramatically by professing, "Not sure what we'd do without you, buddy!"

Julie leaned deeper into the darkness of Kemper, and his arms wrapped her in a bearhug.

I caught Caroline's slight disgust and realized what I already knew. That she was different, not like the other girls. Dufour cracked beers, two at a time, and assigned them to us wayward travelers.

"Not sure we should be walking down the street with those," I said.

"*Boo*," Trumner chided.

"Listen, if you want an envoy to go looking for your ex-boyfriend, there are gonna be stipulations," Bently added.

"Fine," I conceded, taking one of the beers and politely handing it over to Caroline. "But we're cutting through backyards. Need to be a little inconspicuous, alright?"

"Agreed," Trumner said, nodding toward Dufour. "Calm down, donkey."

"Fuck you. I wasn't even doing anything. And I weigh like ten pounds more than you, dick. Call me a fuckin' donkey."

"That's on account of *my* man girth."

"*Ahh, okay.* On that note, I say we head out," Caroline added, playfully using the comment to make an exit. I walked up alongside her and brought up the flashlight to provide a guiding path of light. She laced a hand around my inner elbow, and there was no place else I'd rather have been. Sure, we were looking for Tarkin, and sure, he may or may not suffer from some sort of severe mental illness or something worse, but other than that, nothing seemed better than what I was feeling right then and there.

"Let's go visit Algeir Remington!" Trumner said.

"Excellent idea," Bently followed. "Let's hit The Ridges."

"No," Dufour said. "I don't like that place. Freaks me out."

"Who's Algeir Remington?" Caroline asked.

"You've never heard of Algeir Remington?" Trumner asked. "Dude was a badass."

"Pretty much a professional boxer. Trained at Loral Glove in Cincinnati and was featured in *Sports Illustrated's* 'Faces in the Crowd' section. Pride of Upper Hearth for a few years back in the early eighties. My dad followed him for a bit," I explained.

"Well, how are we gonna visit him?"

"Dude never left The Ridges," Dufour said.

"What's The Ridges?" Caroline asked.

"You'll see," Bently added.

With that, I turned the light toward the woods behind the Herberts' house. Caroline held firm of my hand as I led the group through the woods until we were out on an open patch of grass maybe twenty-five feet by thirty. It was as though a tiny island covered in dirt and clover was raised up from another world. Out beyond was nothing but stars and sky. Caroline walked out ahead of our group a bit and I grabbed her tightly at the elbow. "Be careful. That sky can be disorienting," I said. When I trained the beam of light just ten more feet or so in front of us, she realized what seemed to be more grass was actually the tops of trees. "More than a few people have fallen, Algeir Remington being one of them. Not many people come out here anymore, but in the day it was a pretty prime party spot. It used to be littered with beer cans and fast-food wrappers. And there was talk of Upper Hearth putting up signs and guardrails, but then they realized it was actually still the property of our neighborhood or something. Most people just sort of forgot about it. There used to be a swinging vine that went out over it. Scary as shit. I never did it. And eventually Mr. Mailer chopped it down."

"The tree or the vine?" Caroline asked.

"Oh, sorry, the vine."

We crawled upon our bellies to the edge where the ground turned to treetops. When I shined the beam of the flashlight down inside, Bently pointed out a few reflective eyes and noted the scurry of animals traipsing the avenues of tree branches.

"Pretty rare to get a bird's-eye view of trees," Trumner pointed out.

"No doubt," Caroline said. "We need to come back here during the day. See it in the light sometime. I bet you could lay here for hours watching squirrels and birds."

"Supposedly the creek below is riddled with animal bones," Bently told us.

"Heard the same," Dufour said. "Human too."

"*Oh, bag that shit, Doof. There's no human bones,*" Trumner said. "They didn't leave anyone down there. You can take Caulder Drive all the way in and hike less than a mile. I've been down there. There are animal bones, though."

"From falling from here or out of the trees?"

"No, these are big animals," Trumner continued. "Looked like cow skulls, or sheep. Nobody really has an explanation for it."

"Avril Drummond used to go down there and collect them, use them for art projects and shit, but eventually her parents made her stop."

"She's odd," Bently said.

"You're odd," Dufour followed, pride stretching across his face when Trumner gave him a little nudge for getting a decent dig in on our friend. Such a strange occurrence when Dufour was not the butt of the joke. Something worth celebrating.

"We should get back before Kemper gets Julie pregnant," Trumner said, causing Caroline to roll onto her side in laughter. I pinned her in place with an arm, and it was then that we began laughing again after recognizing how we were on the ledge of a fairly drastic fall.

"Best to get back to stable ground."

But when the rest of the group got to their feet and began to walk away, Dufour stayed in place, fingers over the ledge of the cliff as one might grapple onto a cover pulled up beneath their jaw. "Doof? You comin' big fella?"

I brought the beam of light upon Dufour, but he hardly seemed involved in the present. His body visibly shook, and it looked like you could turn the world upside-down, and he'd likely hold in place exactly how he was then and there. The group approached hesitantly, saying things such as *"All good, big fella?"* and *"Don't wanna add any more skulls to the bottom of that creek, now."* And just as we reached him, he went up on his knees and crawled backwards terrified, knocking Bently's legs out from under him where he landed on his back. "*The fuck, dude?*" Bently said.

But Dufour was going on and on about seeing something in the trees, looking up at him. Only, he could see more than just reflective eyes; this was a face. The face of Algier Remington.

"Oh, come on, man," Trumner added. "The weed's getting to you. And I get it. I totally get it; this strain is from my dad's collection. *Grandpa's Breaths Tar*, it's mostly resin. But get your shit together, dude."

"I'm telling you guys, I fuckin' saw Algier. Fuckin' smiling up at me. Watching me."

"That's it," Bently said as I offered him a hand to help him back up onto his feet. "Back to the homestead. This always happens. Fuckin' biggest dude of us all can't handle his drugs."

SHADOWCASTER

When younger, Kemper, Tarkin, and I would hurry to make it around the neighborhood twice on Halloween. Nearly at a dead sprint, going from house to house with our pillowcases open wide as baby birds. Always ending in Kemper's basement with *Dream Warriors, Evil Dead,* and on one occasion, unforgettable to young boys on the precipice of puberty, *Friday the 13th Part II.* The one where the camera locks in on that girl's ass while she walks through woods before eventually going skinny-dipping. But even in the case of the latter, the focus was on what candy and novelties had been collected. To this day I'm still unable to lose the image of both Kemper and Tarkin sifting through piles of *carpet candy* with wax vampire teeth pegged in their mouths. How uncanny was the play on one's psyche to see young boys dressed up like Indiana Jones and Daniel LaRusso wearing strange waxy teeth. We called it *carpet candy* on account of how it was initially staged before being inventoried and negotiations began. Piles of candy. Milk Duds, Reese's Cups, and Snickers amassed in one pile, Swedish Fish, Jolly Ranchers, and Sour Patch Kids in another. And piles of randos like pretzels, spare change, and an assortment of toys such as witches' fingers and those men with sticky hands and feet that you throw at the wall only to watch them descend back down onto the carpet in a sort of sloppy, uncoordinated crawl. Always leading to one of us inevitably chucking the sucker up onto the ceiling where we would eventually give up on him falling, only to have Kemper tell us his mom got pissed because it left what appeared to be a grease stain from being up there so long. But that was a time of childish things and walking with Caroline and a group of long-time buddies, at least in proximity to my time on this Earth, felt different. Adult. A new stage. Where things seemed more in my control but also seeming to carry more weight.

Trumner and Bently worked hurriedly to shotgun beers before getting back to Kemper's, but Dufour still seemed to be in a world all his own. I unknowingly slapped the handle of the flashlight in the palm of my left hand. Causing Caroline to nonchalantly take it away from me and carry it along her opposite side. The moon was high and bright, and stars pulsed like little earrings in the sky. It had turned out to be a fairly clear and bright night by the standards of late fall, and for that we were unknowingly grateful.

"My cousin and I used to play *Star Wars* when we were little," Caroline said, clicking on the flashlight and brandishing it like a lightsaber. "I was always Princess Leia and she was always Chewbacca."

"That must have been brutal for her confidence," I stated.

"Nah, she was super cute. Still is. Way prettier than me. She just really liked Chewbacca."

"I doubt that."

"No, she did. Could do that throaty voice he made and moved like him and everything."

"No. I mean, I doubt that she's cuter than you."

In that instance I was certain that Caroline had redirected the beam of the flashlight, worried that maybe she was trying to change the subject because I'd embarrassed her. But when I gained my bearings, I realized the light being projected was on a much grander scale, something of which the flashlight we carried was incapable. Our entire group turned toward the light, bringing up the palms of our hands to protect our eyes, but then came the movement of shadows against our persons and above us like a movie projector.

"The fuck?" Trumner asked, drawing the group's attention to the side of the Miosis' house. It was half red brick and half white siding, and the shadowy images played out clearly on both. At first it was intertwined shadowy hands coming together and apart. Forming a bird flying up into the sky, then a dolphin arching up and out of implied water where the brick turned to siding, and then simply a single hand, coming down to meet Dufour's shadow. It was strangely comical, the way the index and thumb latched on to Dufour's shadowy head. Similar to the way someone might unscrew the lid of a bottle. And unscrew is exactly what they began to do. Only, unlike the Dufour that stood beside us, the head of the shadowy Dufour began to rotate, spinning, not once fully around, but twice before the shadowy fingers plucked it loose from its shadowy body. And in one consistent motion, as the shadowy body dropped down into the darkness, the fingers flicked that shadowy Dufour head up and over the roof of the house and out of sight. I looked over at Dufour, who began touching his head to make sure there was a difference between himself and the devastation of the shadow, and he kind of laughed at us as his hands traipsed across the real estate of his head. But before we were able to respond, the shadowy hands went right back into their maligned game, this time forming an image I recognized instantly from my childhood, that of the elephant with an enormous trunk and tusks coming up on each side. And it wasted no time. In one graceful motion, it ducked those tusks low and came up under the shadowy version of Bently, scooping his skinny frame high up across the side of the Miosis' house where he squirmed, clearly displeased with where the tusk had entered his shadowy body, just beneath the ribcage, and where it triumphantly exited past the shoulder blade of his upper back. We watched as Bently's shadow appeared to latch onto the tusk with both hands before sliding down to the base of its slope and eventually going limp. "*This is fucked*," Trumner announced, immediately beginning to retreat from the light.

And that's when we heard it. The sound of tree roots slowly being excavated, popping and bending beyond the parameters of their physical properties. Only it wasn't tree roots we were hearing, but rather the tendons and vertebrae of Dufour's neck and shoulders, fighting with what stubborn anatomy they'd been given to remain in place. Dufour registered widemouthed surprise and eternal shock as some invisible force began to quite literally rotate his head. The life had left him upon the first rotation, but our group knew all too well, just as had been the case for Dufour's shadow, that there would be a second rotation, and it was that very reality that struck us as we began to scream and blood ruptured from the volcano of his carotid artery, painting us all in thick, black blood. Just that quickly, Dufour's head was detached and flicked nonchalantly up onto the roof where it could be heard rolling down the shingles of the Miosis' house before hitting with a dull thud in the grass on the other side. Bently reached out a hand and Trumner took it, grasping a palm against his forearm as though he were trying to pull him from some sort of imaginary water, but his fate was sealed, written upon brick and siding. And just like that, Bently was cast some twenty feet above us where the eventual downward slope of an invisible entity would rearrange his insides.

Our group was raging, running with purposeful pumps of survival, moving our arms and legs just as fast as we could. And when I looked back at the abandoned carnage of our friends, I saw the enormous shadowy hands form the image of the man in the old dirty hat. The one that could smell our fear. The man we'd come to know as Calm Jeffrey. And though the moment was ripe with distraction, I was quite certain the shadowy nose of the man lifted ever so slightly, nostrils flaring, and I could hear that slow, monotone voice say, "*I know. I know. He's coming to see you soon, Bauschy! Your old friend!*"

We hightailed it between the Schoburgs' and Pipers' houses, doing everything in our power to move quickly while also being as quiet as humanly possible. Trumner was crying. We stopped along Ventura Drive and Jamison Court to catch our breath. And Trumner began to cry harder, the type of tears the teen had not likely unleashed since a small boy. Caroline pulled him toward her where muffled tears soaked into the fabric of her t-shirt. When he pulled away, she unknowingly began to wipe a hand over the area in an effort to dry it. I couldn't gain my breath. It was that eternal thrum of terror accompanied by the insistence to run beyond what I'd ever run. Even during soccer two-a-days I didn't feel as worn down as I did in those moments.

"We've got to get back to Kemper and Julie," Caroline told us. "We need to call the police."

But we knew deep down that what the authorities could offer would be of little use. What we witnessed alongside the Miosis' house could not be subdued nor locked away in a cell. It was something beyond understanding. And it was running around the neighborhood, as fucked as that thought even seemed. I peeked my head out from the trees we were standing behind and saw a clear avenue along the fence running parallel to the Bartletts'. An avenue Caroline and I walked hand in hand only an hour or so earlier. I wanted more than anything to be back to that time. A time when our friends were all laughing and breathing and unaware. "On my count," I heard Caroline say. Something that surprised me, not only in the way she took command, but for reasons I never thought would be necessary. "One...two...three..." And though I knew it wasn't coming, I wished more than anything for Trumner to begin fucking with Caroline the way he would in almost any other situation. Saying something to the effect of, *Whoa, whoa, wait! Now, when you say on my count, do you mean go on three? Or three and then go?* But that sort of comedy was lost during such times. Stripped away and likely never to return.

We were back at it, this time anything but quiet, hollering out for Kemper and Julie to be on the ready as we ran toward the house. When we entered the garage, we ripped the door down its tracks, closing ourselves inside. We wanted to holler for Mr. Ellison and his party to *get the fuck moving. Get inside. Waste not another minute. Leave that firepit ablaze, to hell with your drinks and folding chairs and get to safety*, but it all came out in an entangled jumble of grunts and lost breath. So much so that the adults hardly noticed and looked over shaking their heads in that way indicative of adults saying *Kids will be kids.*

Kemper nearly tossed Julie clean off his lap and onto the worn carpet his grandmother willed them. She managed to catch herself by straight-arming the coffee table and grabbing ahold of his shirt. "*The hell, Stanley,*" she barked, seemingly uninterested in the spastic way the rest of the group hurriedly reentered the garage, and more so, disgusted at his inability to protect her in the moment.

"*Guys, what's the deal?*" Kemper hollered.

I stepped down on the aluminum weatherstrip of the garage door, running horizontally to the floor, and locked the waist high handle in place. All three of us were out of breath, and Kemper and Julie were standing up by then, aware that something bad was happening.

"Where's Bently and Doof?" Kemper asked.

But none of us had the breath available to explain. Instead, Caroline pointed to the door leading into the house, and the group followed the nonverbal queue to get inside. Kemper gathered the candles and Julie clicked on the flashlight. A sound that had new meaning.

Inside, Trumner buried his face in the living room sofa, and Caroline and I slid down the wall onto our butts, still working to regain our breath. The backs of our heads leaning against the wall and eyes staring out at nothing, foggy and on the precipice of passing out.

"Seriously, guys. What the fuck's happening?" Kemper asked.

"Yeah, you all are acting crazy."

Trumner moved just enough of his face away from the sofa cushion so that he was able to speak and breathe. *"They're dead! They're all fucking dead!"* Kemper and Julie began asking a litany of questions, all of which went over our heads. We were locked away in that intrinsic neurosis of shock. Survival instincts delivered. Ensured we reached safety before insisting our minds and bodies shut down. Julie went into the kitchen and filled water glasses directly from the tap, dispersing them to each of us and insisting we drink. Caroline's eyes welled with tears as she began to shake her head, clearly wanting to erase what she'd witnessed. I sat with my thighs pulled tightly against my chest, arms wrapped around them. Face buried within the tops of my kneecaps. Body still heaving and attempting to slow its breathing mechanism down to something reminiscent of a baseline. Up the street, through the front windows, laughter could be heard from the adults. *"No, no, no,"* Trumner began, standing and walking over to pound on the window. *"Get inside! You all need to get the fuck inside!"* Kemper went to calm him, but

Trumner was having none of it, pushing Kemper firmly away and raising the window up so aggressively that it bounced at the top of its tracks and nearly closed again. He was insistent they all get inside, screaming like a mad man, but none of them seemed to notice beyond looking down the street at him and continuing on with their conversations. *"What the fuck? Can't they hear me?"* It was then that we heard the subtle sounds of music playing from a radio. Creedence Clearwater Revival. Songs that made us think of war. And the irony was not lost on me and the rest of the group.

"I don't think they can, man," Kemper said. "We need to figure out a way to call the police. Get someone over to check on Bently and Doof."

"You don't understand, man," Trumner insisted. *"They're dead. Fucking dead.* There's nothing to check on! We need to let people know."

"Tarkin killed them," I said.

"It didn't look like Tarkin, man," Trumner followed.

"Yeah, well, I'm not real sure what Tarkin looks like these days. But it was him. Just like we used to see on his bedroom wall when we were younger."

Kemper leaned against the wall, taking in the facts as Julie latched onto him and began sobbing. I knew exactly what Kemper was seeing inside that vacant look. Knew he heard the same voice we spoke of on the school playground after the last time we'd spent the night at Tarkin's. "I'm not going over there anymore," Kemper told me, legs dangling from a swing with his arms wrapped around the chains coming down from the metal rod above. I sat in the one beside him, rocking ever so slightly so that the tips of my toes mimicked that of a ballerina's, making minimal contact with dirt.

"Same," I confessed. "What was that? I mean, how did he do it?"

"Not sure," Kemper said. "But I have no interest in finding out. Something's off, man. Ever since his dad left them. His mom walks around mumbling shit beneath her breath and Tarkin's a zombie. Like he's on another planet. All I know is it feels creepy over there now."

Tarkin's dad used to be engaging and was pretty interactive. When we were young, he used to come home from work to find us sitting in the front yard and would sometimes talk us into an impromptu game of Five Hundred. We would gather at the bottom of the cul-de-sac by Kemper's house as Tarkin's dad rolled up the sleeves of his dress shirt and loosened the noose of his tie. We were not sure if he actually had an arm or perhaps just seemed to on account of us being so young and all, but he would heave that NERF football to mountains' heights and call out *'One hundred...two hundred...three hundred...four hundred...'* or *'Five huuuuuuunreeeed!'* See, the whole idea of the game was that the first to catch the ball and reach five hundred was the winner. Between throws we would mumble things such as "*Where you at? I've got three hundred...*" or "*I had that one, dickhead.*" If you couldn't get to the ball, the least you tried to do was bat it away, so no one else would get the points. It was always a blast. The three of us gathered in a small little horde fighting for an opportunity to catch the ball and impress Tarkin's dad. And he was always so kind. You know, built you up with compliments about the way you hustled or had good hands. The man was all love...until we found that gun in the woods. Kemper was the one who came upon it. We were scouting locations to eat lunch up on Grasshopper Hill when his gym shoe got caught up on the opening lever. And there it was, at least a portion of it, where the barrel selector and comb of the shotgun had been unearthed. We spent the better part of the afternoon working to excavate the gun, working our way around its anatomy with the nose of a shovel and trowel. But once it was unearthed, none of us felt comfortable pulling it up out of the dirt. That's when Mr. Tarkin came into play.

"Tarkin?" Kemper said. "Go get your dad."

Seemed like he didn't necessarily believe us as he was walking up, but shortly thereafter he was saying, *"I'll be damned."* When he picked it up into his hands, the breech opened, as though begging to be loaded. After that he became obsessed. He told us stories of him and his daddy hunting back in the day. He said laying eyes on the gun instantly brought him back to those times. Claimed it was, *"An old FN Browning over/under."* His excitement was extraordinarily heightened, cleaning and refurbishing the gun to damn near its original condition. "See what I'm sayin' about the over/under?" he pointed out, drawing our attention to the fact that the barrels were not side by side but instead one atop of the other. It was as though the gun had unlocked some sort of ancient relic from his past.

After that, most times we saw him he was simply sitting at the kitchen table listening to talk radio and drinking whiskey. Wiping down the gun until it shined. Mumbling to himself and losing color. Only a few weeks after that, he became sick with something. That's when rumors started up about cancer or substance abuse. But we were just unaware at the time. We hadn't realized that we'd unearthed something more than an old shotgun. After he left the family, the gun remained above the fireplace on display, shotgun shells sitting on the mantle.

"Think it's loaded?" Tarkin once asked, but the three of us wanted nothing to do with it.

Adam seemed genuinely afraid. Not due to the gun's natural affiliation toward violence, but perhaps to a past violence he somehow sensed. Some sad history that leaked from its barrels and contaminated the house.

"I almost feel sick when I walk into the house. I'm fine and then I step inside, and I feel like I'm gonna puke."

"Me too. The moment I get back outside I feel fine again. Anyway, just wanted to let you know. I talked to my mom about it a little. Didn't tell her the crazy stuff, not sure she'd believe me anyhow. Heck, I'm not sure I believe it myself. But I'm not going back."

"Me either," I said.

Caroline was at the window, dropping the blinds and then peeking through them. I mustered the ability to get to my feet and join her, noting that she had a sort of innate courage that was somewhat of a rarity for our generation.

"What we need to do is not draw attention. What we saw out there is not something you want to be the focus of," Caroline said.

"Well, what was it?" Julie asked, rubbing her triceps with opposite hands, similar to what people do when cold.

Just then that spotlight appeared around the corner, slowly working its way across the landscape of the neighborhood. Trumner, Caroline, and I responded by crouching down in protective positions, already suffering from the early onset of posttraumatic stress. Julie and Kemper backed away, sort of watching us with the naivete of young people who'd never dabbled in the progressions of distress. The spotlight ran down the neighboring houses and into the front room where our group took refuge. It was not until it passed us and pointed at a downward angle that we realized the police cruiser had returned from earlier. He pulled up to the Ellisons' driveway and spoke with the group. Caroline and I worked up the front room windows and heard the music lower to a whisper, followed by muffled conversation between the officer and neighbors. There was a smidge of laughter, and Mr. Ellison walked up and leaned against the cruiser with both hands braced against the frame. His soft body shook as he nodded in agreement about something, and then he tapped the top of the cruiser in a way that one might when a vehicle is getting ready to pull away. I felt outside of myself. Listening to screams and pleading for help that seemed unnatural, even at such a heightened state. But then came Caroline, and Trumner and even Julie and Kemper doing the same, screaming and pounding on the windows. Julie, now in possession of the flashlight, began to click it on and off, over and over again, in some spastic undisciplined type of Morse code. And just as the officer began to pull forward, heading away from us, his brakes let out a slow squeak, and he and Mr. Ellison looked in our direction. Some other words were exchanged between the two before the officer put it in reverse to come down to the bottom of the cul-de-sac.

There was little urgency to the officer's curiosity, and even as we banged on the window and flashed the light upon ourselves to show him that we were a group of frightened kids, he seemed to be going through the motions. Checking up on an inconvenient disturbance. When he stepped from the vehicle and walked toward the door, we realized he was fairly young and strong. Sort of physique that might have threatened Kemper's manliness and sparked Julie's curiosity in any other situation. But that was another time. Another moment in a world where Adam Tarkin didn't exist. Or was at the very least overlooked by naivete and the pursuits of self-focus.

"Evenin' kids," the officer said. And despite the heightened state of things, I felt myself relax a bit, exchanging a look with Caroline as though it might be okay, that things may be over. My mind even going so far as to think they may have captured Tarkin. Maybe even had him down at the station at that very moment. But they would have no idea what they had. No idea what freakish possibilities were locked away in Tarkin's little body. "You all okay to open the door for a minute? Have a little talk?" Kemper went to open the door but was immediately stopped by Trumner, who barricaded himself in front of it by pinning the weight of his heft against it with a shoulder.

"We can't," he said. "It's not safe."

Caroline seemed to be on the same page and crouched down to speak with the officer through the screen of the open window.

"I'm sorry, Officer," she began. "But we're really scared."

"Totally understand, young lady. But Tri-State Energy is working on getting power restored as we speak. Be a few hours, though. Something got ahold of the pole down the street. Thought maybe a car struck it, but it was something different altogether. Never seen anything like it, to be honest. Entire pole looks like it was ripped down the middle and shredded by some sort of animal or somethin'."

"*Our friends are dead,*" I said, sort of looking toward Caroline and Trumner for approval to share the news.

"Come again?" asked the officer, reaching down now for his flashlight and shining it in my face. "I'm sorry, son.

I think I may have misheard you." But he could tell by the looks on our faces that he'd heard things loud and clear.

"Adam Tarkin," Trumner said. "There's something wrong with him."

But that was all that time would allow. It was in those moments that a bright light appeared on the group of adults up the street. Bright enough that it lit up the houses like sunshine, even from where we watched down in the cul-de-sac. Mr. Ellison walked to the edge of the driveway and began to address whoever it was shining the light as the rest of the group unleashed disgruntled *dudes* and *hey, hey, hey's* while shielding their eyes. "*Easy with the light, pal,*" Mr. Ellison said. But that was all the leeway he was granted. Seconds later, hands came out from either side of the beam and began to manipulate the shadows. There were horrible screams of sickening pain, followed by the pops and tears of bones and tendons. The closest thing us teenage kids would witness to the horrors of war.

The officer stood, frozen and uncertain how to respond. No amount of training had equipped him for such an unimaginable magnitude of violence. Something struck the front of the house and the officer leaned over to have a look, shining a light upon what was clearly a severed finger wearing an enormous championship ring. And then the light went out, and all was silent, save for the subtle cracks and pops of the firepit on the driveway. The officer retrieved his Glock and turned his attention toward the Ellisons' home and slowly walked toward his cruiser. He was in the midst of pulling his radio from the tactical vest when I heard it. Slight, but true. The sounds of my nightmares. The slap of palms meeting solid earth. The officer shined the beam of his flashlight up the middle of the street as a shadowy image padded into view, *slap, slap, slap*.

And then I began to run through the rhyme I'd heard all those years ago in Adam Tarkin's bedroom.

Scottie Mills, the mailman, crawling through your head... Scottie Mills, the mailman, climbing up your bed...it was a car on Blushing Avenue, somebody said...struck and killed the mailman, now he's DEAD! DEAD! DEAD!

Caroline slowly backed away from the window and mumbled, "*Daddy?*" and I knew that numerous nightmares were being inflicted upon us all at once. That what played out before me was separate and personal and unkind. And though the images playing out before us were different, the dangers they carried were eminent and built from malevolence.

Scottie Mills' severed torso trotted down the street with the nonchalance of a canine. His gaze fixed upon the light, coming toward us all. Sinister. Evil. Ready to devour. But the officer stepped toward him and began to speak. Only, what he said seemed dissociated from the visions playing out in my head, and from what I gathered, Caroline's head as well. Because he was clearly speaking to Adam Tarkin, calling out that he *stop right there, turn around and place his hands on his head*. But such requests become impotent when dealing with things beyond this world. Things for which there is little known remedy, ailments that strike the very fibers of human understanding.

And then the officer lowered the gun and spoke of his own sadness. His own nightmare. Corresponding with the traumas of *his* life. Perhaps the loss of a brother? Or someone he'd had to shoot while on duty? Filling another person's body full of holes. Little crescent moons and misshaped bellybuttons. Made no matter. His guard was down, and madness was upon him.

There was the nauseating sound of chewing, something similar to an old person, shed of manners, and when Julie cast the light upon the officer, our entire group watched as Tarkin bit down hard upon the man's jugular and pulled it up and away with the overexertion one might when ripping wires from the walls of a condemned building. There was an initial spray from the external jugular vein, followed by a flow consistent with that of an open fire hydrant. A tide of blood sprung forth and covered the front walkway and porch. The officer struggled momentarily before falling limp as his face registered an eternal state of death.

"Fuck, fuck, fuck," Kemper rattled.

"Close the blinds! Close the blinds, man!" Trumner screamed.

Kemper dropped the blinds, making that aluminum popping sound, as Caroline and I slammed the small portion of the front window we'd raised. Our entire group backed away from the windows as shadows revealed the terror of what was happening outside. Tarkin had not stopped at the severed jugular of the officer but instead continued with his onslaught, as though wanting to send a clear message. Much in the same way we'd watched those shadows cast upon the side of the Miosis' house, we now watched the terrible melee projected upon the front blinds by the officer's discarded flashlight. It rocked ever so slightly, rolling the horrible images upon us as though watching through a broken kaleidoscope. Only, there were no colors. Only black murder. The shadow of a teenage boy pulling intestines and organs loose of a body and holding them above his head, taut and trembling as elastic exercise bands, before discarding them with a dull thud onto the front lawn. Then, as peaceful as a mother turning off a child's bedroom light, the flashlight clicked off and there was only darkness. Our group fought to stifle heavy breathing and screams. Terror lodged in our throats like obstinate little pills.

That went on for quite some time before our group crawled into the kitchen, surrounded by the safety of the cabinets. The very same kitchen we played Hot Wheels in when we were younger. Pretending the slats of the wooden floorboards were roadways we had to stay within. Using Castle Grayskull as a police station, shoeboxes as houses, and a comforter bunched and fluffed perfectly to replicate that of a mountain. How we'd carve details into those shoeboxes with his dad's X-acto knife, punching out windows, and tiny front doors, and of course garages. Garages that raised outward and allowed us to park our Hot Wheels inside.

"*What are we gonna do?*" Julie asked.

"Stay here. Stay together," I said.

"*Are you kidding?* We're sitting ducks here," Kemper told me.

"Well, what the hell else are we supposed to do? *Go out there with that thing?*" Trumner exclaimed.

"What about the cop, right? I mean, how long will they wait to come looking for him when he's not responding?" Caroline asked.

"In Upper Hearth? *Ah, a while.* Nothing ever happens here," Trumner added.

She looked over to me, and I could only shrug and admit it could be a while. That's when we heard the staticky squawk of the officer's radio on the other side of the door. Perhaps if we could simply get out the door, a mere five feet to where the officer was laying, we could use his radio to call for help? In order to do this successfully though, we decided that Kemper would go out after the radio, with me directly behind as a sort of spotter. Julie would remain in the front room and open and close the door while Caroline watched through the blinds of the front window. As an added precaution, Trumner would go up to Kemper's room, located at the front of the house, for a bird's-eye view. But that took a little convincing, as Trumner wanted no part of being away from the group, at least not an entire floor away.

"*Dude, don't be a pussy,*" Kemper said to him.

"*I can't take you calling me a pussy right now.*"

"*Okay, I'm sorry.* Look, man. We need you and you've got this. You're the biggest and strongest of all of us," Kemper said. Kemper was a natural leader, and at times, genuinely caring. He locked a hand around the back of Trumner's neck and brought their foreheads together. "You can do this. Besides, a predator naturally goes for the weakest link. If any of us should be nervous right now, it's Bauschy." The two looked to me as I shook my head and slightly smirked before the seriousness of the situation regained our attention. "It will be seconds, if that, and we will be on the horn, callin' in the troops. Promise." Trumner nodded his head and stopped to take in the scene for a moment longer. After that, he nodded his head some more, as though telling himself, *Okay, okay, fuck it, let's get this done,* and took to the steps, each one groaning with the presentation of his weight.

Caroline went to the blinds and looked out into the open, empty night. The firepit up at the Ellisons' was actively dying, giving the Tarkins' house across the street a sort of fluttering look, as though the house was moving to the nuances of the flames. She looked over at Kemper and I, who were crouched on one knee with the other foot planted and ready to go once given the all clear. Above us, Julie manned the door, awaiting the nod to whip it open and quietly close it while we worked. Trumner creaked the floorboards above and we could hear the blinds bend when he pulled them down for visibility. He knocked on the floor, causing the rest of us to nearly piss ourselves, which in turn led to us using numerous expletives and losing focus.

"What the fuck, Trumner?" Kemper whisper-yelled up the steps behind us.

"My bad," a yell-whisper responded. "All good. I don't see shit."

Kemper and I locked eyes and nodded before giving Julie the green light. She threw the lock and opened the door just wide enough for the two of us to exit before slamming it shut, as quietly as possible, behind us. Outside, crickets chirped, and moths bucked off the outside lights, begging entrance. And perhaps that's all their little lives consisted of, simply going toward the light. I crouched behind Kemper as we both duckwalked quickly toward the officer. His condition was much more grotesque than we'd imagined, and Kemper began to openly dry heave. He brought the neckline of his t-shirt up and housed his nose and mouth inside, like a robber hiding his identity. There was a moment when he placed a hand down to gain balance and slid down onto his elbow. It was unclear whether he'd put his weight on a spleen or a portion of liver, but the consistency looked to be that of a mossy sponge.

His hands sifted through the sludge of the officer's insides, frantically hunting for the radio. And then it came, a call muffled beneath the officer's armpit area and back, where the coiled jumper cord had wrapped and tangled. "*Unit 7 checking status of Unit 5. Unit 5,*" the corresponding officer asked, "*please state location and status.*" Kemper sifted through the mess of man frantically, as I brought a hand upon his shoulder and continued to keep my head on a swivel. Reminded me of my dad talking about Priest Holmes. *You should see him, he'll literally put a hand on one of his lineman's shoulders, sort of like the fella is an escort, and then BAM, he sees a hole open up and he's gone. Really somethin'. Really somethin' to see.* I wished my dad was with me then, watching the madness that was taking place, guiding me until I could find a hole and run. And that's what I wanted to do. As cowardly as it sounded. I wanted to run. Book it right up the street and home to my mom and dad. But before I was able to act upon such a thought, I heard the soft sound of bare feet walking down the street. I located the officer's long handle flashlight and shined it in the direction the sound was coming from to witness Adam Tarkin slowly walking toward us. There was no expression upon his face; in fact, it appeared as though he were in some sort of trance. He wore a t-shirt and flannel pajama pants and above all else, was covered in the officer's blood. But there was no aggression to him at all. As though he was a wild animal who'd had its fill. No longer hungry.

"Do you think he recognizes us?" I asked.

"Are you fucking serious right now?" Kemper responded, looking up momentarily before going beneath the police officer as if the man was an enormous stone blocking an exit we desperately needed to escape through. *"Help,"* was all he was able to muster as I laid the flashlight at an angle that kept Tarkin within its beam. After that, I got beneath the officer's waist and located a belt loop to assist with rolling him over. Kemper immediately located the radio and began sounding the alarm. *"We need help! 3307 Candlemaker Drive, officer down! Repeat, officer down!"*

There was pounding on windows and screaming from our three friends inside the house. Caroline even went so far as to raise the window and punch out the screen as another option for us to get back inside. And that's when I saw it, like a beacon in a black ocean, the sheen fiber optic rods of the Glock. I grabbed it and pointed it toward Adam Tarkin, but my old friend was nowhere to be found. Only empty street. But there was something in the darkness on the side of the house, hidden but clearly close enough to strike. Kemper worked to remove the radio from the officer's vest, but the base of it seemed to actually be stitched within the fabric.

"We've got to get him closer to the house," Kemper said as I tucked the Glock in the waist of my jeans and immediately went back to the officer's waistline and took ahold of his belt for leverage. Portions of the man fell away as we began to heave him backward in an undulating motion, and I was both surprised and sickened by how light he was on account of what portions of his body were no longer attached. And then the light was upon us. Like a spotlight upon convicts during a prison break. Blinding the two of us. Forcing us to look down at our feet.

"Inside," Caroline screamed as the door swung open with a pop.

Both of us didn't so much as rush into the house as fall back into it the way you might when playing tug-o-war and the other team lets go of the rope. Julie instantaneously slammed the door shut, and right on cue, the light from outside went out. There was nothing more than our breathing again until *"Unit 7, requesting status of Unit 5. Come in Unit 5, over."* Kemper looked down and seemed astonished to find that he'd held onto the radio, its coiled cable stretched to its limits, so much so that it appeared one straight line, pinned between door and frame. *"We're here. We're here,"* Kemper began shouting. And then came the sick sad sound of a barber's shears and the cord popped from the doorway, curling like a pig tail. Kemper looked down at his hand, deflated, before throwing the radio aggressively against the wall. *"FUUUUCK."*

I found Caroline in a corner near the back of the room, hugging her knees, huddled in a ball, staring blankly. Rocking, ever so slightly, self-soothing, working to calm herself from the atrocities she'd witnessed. As though once Kemper and I were back inside, the seriousness of the situation paralyzed her ability to function on the most basic level. I placed a palm on each shoulder and tried to get her to focus on me. *"What did you see?"* I asked, but she seemed completely oblivious to external influence. *"Caroline! I need you to look at me! Need you to focus! Now, what did you see?"* But it was not so much *what* she saw, as *who* she saw, and I knew the answer before she even opened her mouth. She'd seen her father. Assuredly as I'd seen Scottie Mills the mailman, she'd seen her father. Only, what she described was a monster of an event. Just as he'd done in the hospital those months leading up to his death, she said he was walking down the street while the officer shined a light and ordered him to stop, carting along that IV stand, its wheels squeaking that awful high-pitched way they had in the hallways of Mercy Hospital. How she hated them, those swiveled wheels *squawking* each time her father found the strength to walk twenty feet to the ice machine or get up to use the restroom. And just as he had in those days, he wore nothing but that faded and soiled hospital gown. She'd seen him nude on a few occasions when the hospital gown opened at an inopportune time, turning her head while her mother lovingly chastised him, "Now, Lonnie, we've got to be aware with our Line visiting." *Line* was the nickname they'd given her when she was just a baby and would be the last word she'd heard him speak before taking his final breath. And that's what she claimed he was saying as his tired bones walked down the street. Just as he had that day, but instead of once, he said it over and over, barely audible, as though a cacophony of dust were accompanying it, *Line...Line...Line...*as he let go of the IV stand, causing it to go down on its side and drag along behind him until ripping loose from his arm. "*Caroline,*" I said, more boldly than I'd meant, but also wanting to ensure I had her attention. "*It wasn't him. Okay? I promise. It wasn't him.*" And then she was in my arms, crying, producing the type of tears that accompany perpetual heartbreak, while clinging and pulling at my t-shirt. I shushed her in a comforting way, pulling her close, knowing that she saw images of her father tearing at that officer's skin, pulling at his insides and focusing one exquisite bite upon the man's neck. Same events I'd seen Scottie Mills deliver upon the sorry soul. Only, more personal. Harder terror.

"It's true," Kemper said, drawing all attention. "Just like Tarkin told us when we were kids...he can smell our fear."

Julie began to speak but swallowed her words, wanting to accuse the group of being off their rockers but clearly playing through the events of the night and becoming increasingly aware that what she thought was reality had diminished. Trumner came flying down the steps, the way one does when they kind of get scared and speed up at a faster pace than their body might be prepared to move. I remember doing that with the old auxiliary fan built into the upstairs ceiling of our house when my mother would say, "Honey, be a doll and run up and flip the fan on, would ya?" How the grated slats laid flush upon the ceiling as I made my ascent up the carpeted staircase, knowing that the second I flipped that switch they'd open up and go vertically, like long, thin razorblades as the growl of the fan chased me down the steps and back to the safety of our family room. Trumner moved with that same sort of conviction.

"Trumner," I asked, "what did you see?"

"Just Tarkin, man. Not sure there's anything I fear more than that little fucker at the moment."

"Maybe we're safe in here? With the blinds drawn? Away from the light?" I began to say. "I mean, you all saw it. The second we got inside that light went out. So, for now, let's just stay away from the windows. Stay out of sight."

"That's the plan? Stay put. Stay out of the light?" Julie complained. The statement seemed contradictory to dispelling evil. Weren't we always taught to step into the light, or at least toward it?

"I'm not sure we have any other choice," I told her.

Caroline stood up and walked into the kitchen, drug two chairs from the table behind her, and shoved one up under the front door handle, wedged it in place, front legs in the air while the back dug firmly into the hardwood. She kicked at the legs, knocking them firmly into place for reassurance before going to what she figured to be the basement door and doing the same. "There's not even outside access down there," Kemper said, but she didn't seem to care, kicking at the chair just as she had the other only moments before. I began to follow suit, placing a chair in the same fashion against the door leading out to the garage before recruiting Trumner to help me flip the kitchen table up onto its side to block the patio entrance. And then we were at it, moving the couch over and stacking the loveseat and end tables to block the front window. Unplugging and moving the refrigerator from the wall to block a side window, making its weight useful. Rolling up floormats and wedging them beneath the refrigerator's small wheels to ensure the unit wouldn't budge.

Afterwards, we found ourselves once again, huddled against the kitchen cabinets, staying down and out of sight. None of us spoke, seemingly alone with our fear. In the hour or so since losing power, our pupils dilated and retinas became more sensitive to low-light conditions, allowing us to nearly make out one another's features. Or perhaps that was the mind filling in the gaps? Providing sadness to Caroline's big brown eyes and severity to Trumner's thick, pursed brow. Or that strange grin that I began to note upon Julie's slim face, corners of her lips reaching high arches upon her cheekbones as her chin began to elongate. *Or was she changing? Right before my eyes? Becoming something else? Something with the ability to maim and murder?* And I was almost convinced that she was, just about to say as much to the group, when we heard the gentle rap upon the glass of the back door, followed shortly thereafter by the hushed tones of someone talking.

"Fuck's that?" Julie asked. And just that quickly her features turned back to that of my scared friend. She looked to Kemper for comfort and explanation, but he simply shook his head as an indication that he was just as curious as she was. She nudged Kemper to go have a look and he volunteered that I should go with him. Kemper reached behind me and retrieved the Glock from

my waistline, where I'd completely forgotten to have put it.

"For shit's sakes, dude, that makes me really uneasy," Trumner said.

"As opposed to what? Our childhood friend going on a fucking rampage? Or maybe the fact that shadows are actually tearing our neighbors apart? Me loading this gun is one of the more normal things you're gonna see tonight."

Once again came the *tap, tap, tap* upon the glass door, only this time it sounded familiar, as though the mention of neighbors somehow evoked one to make an appearance. As simple as a neighborly knock upon the glass. So much so that I genuinely awaited a request for a cup of sugar or a hand moving a couch. We approached the upturned kitchen table cautiously, going low on either side to peek around the sharp corners.

"*Well, who is it?*" Trumner asked.

"Mr. Ayres," Kemper said. "He's got blood all over him."

I listened as the rest of the group immediately went into the debate of letting him in as opposed to keeping that door locked and blocked. Caroline was of the mind that we should let him in, and Kemper clearly was too, as he began sliding the table away from the doorway. But Trumner and Julie were of a different mind, one that preferred they proceed with restraint and consider the possibility that by letting the man in, there might also be the potential of letting something else in. "*Wait*," Trumner begged, once again pinning the table in place with a shoulder, causing the table to shift slightly, allowing us to see the fear on Mr. Ayres' face. He was pleading that we open the door and let him in. Looking over his shoulder frantically, terrified of whatever it was he thought might be coming for him. His desperation was exasperated the moment he made eye contact with Kemper and I, which caused us to look at one another and nod in agreeance that we should let him in. "All I'm saying is we need to consider an alternative, man. Weigh the pros and cons here?"

"*Trumner*," Kemper said, "he's gonna fuckin' die out there, man."

"Maybe? You don't know *for sure*, though!"

"*Get the fuck out of the way,*" Kemper demanded.

"He's right," I said. "We have to consider what we might be opening ourselves up to."

"*So, what? We're gonna let a man die?*"

Julie was actively shushing the man, trying to get him to be reasonable and stay quiet, but the moments were beyond reason, and the man was beginning to panic something fierce. Moments away from grabbing patio furniture and violently forcing his way in. That's when Caroline stepped up to the door, so close that her breath fogged the glass.

"Mr. Ayres, I need you to listen. Go to the front of the house. As quietly as you can. We're going to open the garage door and let you in."

He refuted the option briefly before his eyes registered what she was saying. As the man stepped away from the glass and began to nod in understanding, a long line of bloody saliva stretched from his lip down onto the patio. And, as he headed around to the front of the house, she explained to us that this was a way we could let him in safely and also avoid the risk of opening up the house. As she said this, she walked into the front room and kicked the chair loose from where it was wedged beneath the door handle leading out to the garage. I worked in concert with her, immediately going out into the garage, cracking the lock on the overhead garage door before running back inside. I heard the man immediately begin to lift the door up its tracks, felt it going up above me like an enormous wave. Followed by the man's desperation, begging that I *wait, wait, wait*. Pleading that we just let him inside with the rest of us, but just that quickly we had the interior door closed and locked, pinning the chair back in place. The man's weight slammed against the door as he began pounding and screaming that we let him in before resigning to the fact that this was as good as it was gonna get. We then heard him struggle to walk over to the garage door and pull it down its tracks and click the lock in place. The effort was clearly beyond his comfort level, considering his condition, and he wept and moaned outwardly as he completed the task. Caroline and I stared at each other, breathing heavily, taking solace in the fact that we were at least able to do that. That no matter how things played out for the man, we were at least able to do that.

"We can't leave him out there," Kemper said. *"He's hurt."*

I brought up a hand and told the group to be quiet. Just give things a moment to settle. On the other side of the door, we could hear Mr. Ayres in such a way that made it clear his weight was against the door, likely sitting on the two steps leading into the house with his back against the door. He was mumbling to himself, but we couldn't quite understand what he was saying. All we could make out was that he was openly apologizing for something, as though working to consolidate his sins. There was a strange uneasiness to it all, hearing the only adult in our presence weeping and broken.

"Mr. Ayres, sir? Can you hear me?" I asked. "Are you hurt? We want to help, we're just... we're scared is all."

"I say we open it," Kemper said. "He's locked in there. There's no threat."

"*Just hold up a second,*" I said, putting a hand up. "*Stop talking.*"

"She's, she's after me," Mr. Ayres' muffled voice said from the other side of the door. "She killed them all. *They're all dead.*" With that last emission he sort of laughed and wept. Not the sort of laughter that comes with something humorous or entertaining, but rather when what you once believed is hijacked by the unimaginable.

"Mr. Ayres, we can't understand you. Who? Who did that? Who's after you?"

"*Angel Donnelly,*" he said. "She looked the way she must have when they found her."

And that name struck a nerve with our entire group. We'd all grown up with stories of Angel Donnelly, the girl who'd taken her life when our parents were in high school. Used as an example to be kind. I remembered my own mom using the girl as a talking point on bullying and rumors, teaching me that it was never okay to mistreat your classmates. "That's what happened to Angel Donnelly when we were kids. Bunch of footballers made up stories about her. Saying she allowed them to do certain things." She always used terms such as *footballers* or *jockeys* when speaking of athletes in high school. I was never certain as to why, but my mom being more focused on studies led me to believe that perhaps she wasn't always treated the best by those types and had built somewhat of an aversion to them in general. "Said things about her that were untrue, but word spread like wildfire and her mind was weakened by the constraints of a small community. She'd hung herself in a tree off Sutton Road. Rumors and mistreatment can do a great deal of harm. Always consider such things." And just as we probably all had, I sat up in bed at night and considered my daily transgressions. *Was I kind enough today? Did I find that one kid in need of a friend? Was anything I said mean or hateful?* At times, going so far as to scream out to my parents from beneath my sheets after I'd sworn to have seen Angel Donnelly hanging from the rod of my open closet. And I'd always felt, in regard to keeping kids on the up and up, that story likely worked. Made me consider the possibility that I might even present such an example to my children one day. Something that may guide them down a proper path. But hearing that name again was horrifying. Knowing that Mr. Ayres watched Angel Donnelly revisit her classmates out on the Ellisons' driveway, watched something as horrifying as what Caroline, Trumner, and I saw visited upon Bently and Dufour. Debilitating fragments of fear consolidated within the bosom of the hippocampus. Type of memories that never leave you. Ensure you rarely live another normal day.

"We never meant it to go that far," Mr. Ayres said, mumbling and sobbing. "She was looking me right in the eye as she did those things. Shadows everywhere, moving all around us. And then they were all dead. Nothing but heaps of body parts. *Sounds of soup.*"

Caroline and I nodded in agreement, and then me and Kemper prepared to open the door and get the man inside. He seemed to be in a state of delirium, as though portions of those moments were pulsing in and out like visions on one's deathbed. When we pulled the door open, the weight of the man spilled across the threshold and into the front room. Kemper and Trumner each got beneath an arm and slid the man across the floor as we got under his legs. His abdomen was wide open, and portions of his intestines belched forth like the innards of an overcooked hot dog. He sort of cupped them with his bloodied hands as though trying to keep them inside. The ring finger of his right hand relegated to nothing more than tendons where the finger had been torn free. Julie screamed, closing the door leading out to the garage and throwing the bolt. The man's eyes were nearly rolled up in his head and beads of sweat worked down from his hairline. It was a hard thing to witness. Out of all the adults in the neighborhood, Mr. Ayres was the most well-maintained in both physical health and vanity, with a thick head of hair and healing blue eyes. Strong body built by consistent gym visits and a jawline of chiseled stone. Seeing him reduced to such frailty was incredibly unsettling. Whatever battle was raging within him seemed destined to play out in death's favor.

Caroline and Kemper went upstairs to get clean towels and instructed Julie and I to go into the kitchen cabinet where his mother kept the medical supplies. We came back with tiny strips of gauze that were of little use and stuck to the man's wounds like toilet paper might to a freshly shaved face. He moved bloodied hands across his midsection and every so often seemed to come back into his right mind, going wide-eyed and pale and pinching hunks of intestine between his remaining fingers, trying to work them back beneath the surface of skin. But it was of little use; the intestine slipped from his grasp and seemed to only frustrate him. One of the few things he'd dealt with in his adult life for which he could find no solution. Caroline covered the man's midsection with a clean towel and worked a cool, wet washcloth along the ridge of his brow. She was caring and patient and all the things you would want from someone when in such a situation. There were times Mr. Ayres would look to her with the fear of a child, and she would say things such as *Shh, shh, shh, it's all okay, you're gonna be okay*, but we knew that he wouldn't. Knew that Caroline was saying things as genuinely as she could, fully aware that he was going to die. And I loved her for that. Providing comfort to a stranger in a time of uncertainty, when he was reduced to nothing more than a fearful child, and she was forced to step into a role she'd yet to play.

"Caroline?" Julie said, the look in her eyes indicating she was deep in thought. But Caroline was too focused on Mr. Ayres to respond. "*Caroline?*" she called out again in a sad, fearful voice.

"*What?*" Caroline responded, showing the first signs of frustration.

"My mom's coming," Julie said. "She's supposed to pick us up."

WAITIN' ON THE REAPER

It had become more than apparent that what was hounding us was death itself. Brought onto us by collected fear and past transgressions. Julie looked scared, sick even, and though I would come to dislike her later in life, I felt sorry for her then. Respected the genuine concern she had for her mom. They were best friends in a way, something which seemed a bit toxic in their case but worked for others. Some strange social construct that could shape one kid into a terrible human while allowing another to turn out swimmingly. And perhaps it had less to do with the friendship and more to do with the parent. From what I gathered, it wasn't so much the relationship she had with her mom, but the person her mom was. Either way, the wrong person died that night.

Kemper's dad had a roll of reflective tape in the garage from when he redid the drive way, used it to keep anyone from pulling in until the cement had dried. Caroline and Julie used the tape to showcase words of warning on the upstairs windows. A message that might present itself when headlights shined upon it. Julie sobbed while working portions of tape away from the roll per Caroline's direction. Kemper rubbed her back in an attempt to provide comfort. Such a strange state of affairs, two people who'd likely be nothing more than a blip on each other's adolescent radars, pushed toward a place of primordial survival. Caroline was focused and driven to lay out the messages quickly and clearly. Something that would garner immediate and direct attention. It was due to that thought process that she told Julie she'd be spelling out her mom's first name, *NORMA*, followed by the simple direction, *STOP*. The first window of Kemper's parents' bedroom would read that, with the words in a column, one on top of the other. While the second window said, *GO BACK*. In the windows of Kemper's room, the messages read, *GET HELP* and *LEAVE NOW*.

"Okay," Caroline said. "Now pull the curtains to make the words stand out."

Kemper and I did as she asked, pulling the curtains shut with a *wisp* just as the light clicked on and shined upon us.

Julie muttered, "*Is it her? Is it my mom?*" but she knew who it was. After a moment or so Trumner hollered up from where he peeked through the blind's downstairs, saying that we'd better get those windows covered. Kemper shook his head in a *No shit, Sherlock* kind of way as Julie climbed up onto Kemper's bed and brought her knees up and hugged them close. She unknowingly began sucking her thumb and had teeth that indicated she was once a thumb sucker, you know, front teeth that came out at you a bit when she spoke. Caroline climbed up on the bed next to her and hugged her with motherly conviction.

"I don't even know what time it is," Kemper said, more as an omission on his inability to equate time to the events of the evening than anything else.

"*Ah, guys?*" Trumner yelled up the steps. "*Pretty sure dude's dead.*"

We all stared at one another, none of us wishing to go down and witness what we knew to be inevitable. Caroline was able to get him to rest a bit, but he was still feverish, and we could only do so much to stop the bleeding. In the end, there was communal guilt. And though we knew there were little to no options, there was still the thought that we could have done more, had we the courage. When I removed the blankets and checked Mr. Ayres' pulse, it was apparent he was gone. His skin was pale except for purplish areas around his lower abdomen and the backs of his shoulders where blood pooled beneath his flesh. His lips were flaky, and skin broke off with the blanket when pulled away.

"Should we say a prayer or somethin'?" Trumner asked.

"Yeah," I said. "If anyone knows one?"

We all gathered around Mr. Ayres and bowed our heads. Caroline recited The Lord's Prayer and worked the sign of the cross above the man while we held hands in solidarity. I'm not sure I'd ever prayed up until that point. And though it brings about a bit of shame, not sure I have since. I just never had a notion of where to begin. But, in those moments, I felt the power of Caroline's conviction. She was speaking to a God I'd never truly considered, as though she had a direct pipeline. Had his ear. And then Kemper was covering the man with a sheet he'd gathered from the linen closet. His eyes, not open, but more sort of squinting, as though trying to ignore death's approach. Or a child feigning sleep when a parent sticks a head in to check on them.

"Shit seems so final," Trumner said.

"Yeah," Kemper followed.

Our group stood and crouched around the shrouded body of Mr. Ayres. Just a random man in the neighborhood, one who'd rode past us and waved when we were young and running the streets, playing batter on the bounce or ghost in the graveyard. Same man we'd rode past on our bikes while he was mowing his lawn. Who held boring conversations with our parents in the driveway while we vied for attention. Simply void of life. Such a weird thing to grasp.

"It is, right?"

"What?" Kemper asked.

"Final, I mean," Trumner mumbled. "I don't know, this night's just fucked and shit. I mean, he'll stay dead, right?"

"He's gone," Kemper explained, clearly on the cusp of losing his patience. "Not coming back."

"Okay, good," he said. "I mean, not *good*. I'm not glad he's dead, just not sure we can take much more, right? And now that he's dead, it's probably best he stay that way."

"Probably best you stop talking," Kemper added.

"Yeah. Okay. Cool," Trumner conceded.

"And you know I mean that in the nicest way possible, brother?" Kemper said, lovingly putting a hand on Trumner's shoulder. "I do. I honestly do."

"*Of course. No. I get it.*"

"*Hey,*" Julie said. She stood by the front window with a portion of the loveseat moved, bending a blind. Kemper and I worked to bring the furniture away so we could all have a look. What we witnessed was Mrs. Tarkin standing in the open doorway of her home, candle in hand, brightening her features. A tunneling hallway of darkness behind her. She was shrouded in that same blanket the Steimles' had draped upon her shoulders, hunched forward to keep it in place.

Moments later, she stepped from the house and began whaling on the rope of the bell. Ringing it for all to hear. Adam walked toward her from across the street, as though some villainous creature returning home after a hard day's work. She reached up to adjust the blanket with her free hand, pulling it snuggly in place over her shoulders. When Adam reached her, she took his face into her hands and brought her forehead against his, saying something we were unable to make out. Adam removed her from his path, aggressively taking hold of her by each arm and moving her out of his way. He then stepped into the house and closed the door while Mrs. Tarkin went down to her knees in the grass.

"What the fuck was that?" Trumner asked.

"Maybe he's tired?" I offered.

"We really need to consider this as an opportunity to get the fuck out of here," Caroline said.

"*Yes*," Trumner agreed, pointing a finger at her. "*What she said.*"

We devised a plan that left me keeping watch from the front window while the rest of the group brought the barricade down from around the sliding glass door of the back patio. Julie stepped behind the group as they worked, clearly panicked, and began to insist they stay put on account of her mom coming to pick her and Caroline up. Kemper tried to reason with her, stating we needed to get out before Tarkin came back out of that house. There were no two ways about it, we couldn't risk being trapped any longer and needed to go find help. But it was of no use. She sat down, deflated and weeping. Utterly broken. There was a side of her that wanted to run, but the love she had for her mother was admirable, and she was unwilling to let her walk right into a trap.

"She'll see the signs," Kemper insisted. "And when she does, she'll go to the police."

"No. No. I can't. I can't leave. *That's it. I just can't.*"

And then fate decided for us. I bent back the blinds to allow headlights to shine in. The group walked over to the window slowly and watched as her mom's car paused at the top of the street. She was outside the car at that point, merely one step into the street with the driver's side door open. Her attention focused on the Ellisons' driveway, trying to get a read on what it was she was seeing. That's when we began pounding on the windows. She looked our way and hurried to get back in the car. She started down the hill and then stopped again, registering our frightened group in the window but also noticing the messages above us. She sort of did that thing people do when they pull up to a stoplight and kind of have to lean forward in order to see the light. And then she put that car in reverse and began backing up. Julie sighed with relief, knowing that her mother was doing as they insisted and leaving to go get help. There was a synergistic energy in the air. A reprieve. A feeling that all this horror might be coming to an end as that Audi backed up and around the corner, out of sight. But just as quickly as it disappeared, it reappeared, idling at the stop sign where a left turn would bring her back down the cul-de-sac to us. It was odd watching the car. Not seeing it so much as Julie's mom, but some sort of animal completely confused as to what its next move should be. As a deer might register unexplainable salience in their environment. Whispers of a threat. And then she was coming down the street, scraping her bumper as she came up onto the driveway.

When Julie opened the door, her mom was already standing on the front walkway above the remains of the officer. She cried out to her mom and ran into her arms, sobbing.

"*It's okay,*" her mom said. "*It's okay, I'm here.*"

She was thin, like Julie, though much shorter than I would have imagined. It was rumored she was a hardnosed lawyer for McAleavy and Dunn out of Cincinnati and involved in smear campaigns against numerous small businesses, but the details were unknown to us. She was dressed in a bathrobe and house slippers, clearly not anticipating a need to get out of her vehicle and be seen.

"Mom, it's the kid up the street. The one everyone's been talking about..."

The front door to the Tarkins' house opened quickly with an unnerving *thud*. Our attention was drawn, staring at the open black hole of the doorway. Julie began to lead her mom back to the car and insisted she climb in. Urged us all to follow, but most of us were frozen in anticipation of what would come next. And then he appeared, the same small-framed boy we'd seen wreak havoc upon the neighborhood. He walked toward us with innate, mechanical focus. As though coming after us was simply written in the laws of the land. An act beyond his control. His mom called out to him from the doorway, as simply as a mom telling her child that it was getting late and best to come inside, but it made no matter. Trumner stood in the doorway of Kemper's house looking back and forth between Tarkin coming down the street and where Mr. Ayres lay dead on the floor. I assured him that what he was seeing wasn't real. It was merely a play upon his fear. "Remember," I told him, "you were just talking about Mr. Ayres *staying* dead. Well, he is. That's not him, man. It's meant to cripple you. Don't let it."

We rushed over to the Audi and began to force ourselves inside. Julie hopped in the front and Kemper opened the door to allow Caroline into the back. That's when the beam of light fell upon us. Shadows scattered and I was knocked from my feet. Batted away as simply as one might swat a housefly, laying me flat upon the front lawn struggling to gain my breath. The wind knocked clean from my body and my head throbbing where it connected with solid earth. I heard screams and Kemper cursing Tarkin. Calling out in declaration that he was going to *fuck him up*. And then there was the silhouette of Kemper running toward the light, rushing with the ferocity of a wild animal. Julie's mom backed out from the driveway and overcorrected. The car stopped behind Kemper, not wanting to hit him, as he ran up the middle of the street. Such an anomaly, witnessing Tarkin's harmless little hands come out in front of that beam of light. Knowing the power they possessed. Caroline screamed first, followed by the horn from the Audi—a sissified, audible *meeeeeep* that cut into the night. Perhaps that was the only solution Julie's mom could offer at the time, but it made no matter.

Kemper was hoisted high by two enormous, shadowy hands, each pinching him at a wrist, crucified in midair, elongated like a Stretch Armstrong doll. Until the head of each humerus separated from the sockets of his shoulders and his body dropped down into the street. Julie screamed from within the car as an enormous black fist came down upon the front hood and caused the wheels and frame to momentarily leave the street. Then the Audi was rolling backward, down the cul-de-sac and into the side yard of Kemper's house, past where I lay in the grass. I saw the horrified look on Caroline's face as she worked to open the door, but to no accord. The car rolled down the hill along the side of the house and out of sight.

Trumner was under my arm, pulling me to my feet and leading us around the side of the house. The car sat at an angle at the bottom of Kemper's steep backyard with the headlights pointing up into the night sky. The tail end nestled into overgrowth from the woods where it dipped into the small creek bed. There was no longer light behind us where Kemper's maimed body lay. And it was weird; I wouldn't say that what I was feeling was terror or fear at that point, but more concern. Overwhelming concern.

Save for the hiss and ping of the cooling engine, there was only silence. No one moved from inside the car. Trumner let loose of me and rushed down into the woods, knocking tree branches from his path like annoying turnstiles. I rushed to the best of my ability, still foggy and slightly nauseous.

"*They're alive*," Trumner called to me.

Caroline pushed the back door open with her legs to combat the added pressure from the shrubbery, as Trumner leaned into Julie's window, taking her face in his hands and reassuring her, "*You're good. You're okay.*"

Tarkin stood at the top of the hill, his silhouette in communion with the hulking shadow of the house. Trumner and I scrambled to get the doors open to free Julie and her mother, but they were barricaded in by foliage and trees. Julie fought against the odds, notching the bark of one of the trees with the metal edge of the door before trying to squeeze her thin frame out the slight opening. Caroline directed them both to climb over the seats and exit out the back as she had, but their movements were stunted and dazed from the trauma of the impact. That's when something strange happened. Tarkin stood a mere ten feet from where the car was embedded in the woods and creek, simply staring at us.

"*Easy, Tarkin,*" I said. "*Take it easy, man.*"

Tarkin's features were elongated in shadow but hard to make out in the darkness. There seemed no desire to pursue us any further. He stood there craning his neck back and forth as might an animal who didn't understand. And we didn't understand either, because we were more vulnerable than we'd been all night. Exhausted and broken and ready to fold. Still, there was no effort toward violence. The flashlight remained at his side, no thought of bringing it up and clicking it on. Something had changed. And then he simply turned around and started back up the hill. He simply walked away.

Caroline and I helped Julie and her mother over the seats and out the back door as Trumner stepped up into Kemper's yard, stupefied as to what was going on. And as soon as his foot crossed the threshold, Tarkin turned on a dime and began his pursuit, bringing that beam of light upon him. Trumner cowered in fear and stumbled back into the woods, and just as quickly, the light clicked off, and Adam Tarkin once again began to walk away.

"*What the fuck is goin' on?*" Trumner asked.

"I don't know," Caroline said. "But we need to get the hell out of here."

I was clearly still trying to gain my bearings, leaning my weight against a tree. "You all follow the woods down onto Clough Pike and take it to get help. I'm gonna go make sure my mom and dad are okay."

"*Dude,*" Trumner began, "*let's just get out of here. We can bring help for them. Come on, man.*" This coming off more like a child begging, on account of him hopping slightly up and down in a sort of tantrum. But there was no telling how long it would take them to get to the main road and on into town.

"I can't. They may have no idea any of this is even going on."

"I'll go with you," Caroline said. I looked her in the eyes and saw there would be no persuading her otherwise, before nodding in agreement.

"Okay," I said. "You guys go get help. We'll see you soon."

Trumner put an arm on my shoulder and nodded as he accepted the separation. It was difficult, considering the possibility we may never see each other again, but then Julie's mom took her hand and began leading her down through the woods. She reached up and tugged at Trumner's shirt tail, indicating he needed to come along.

SOUNDS OF SOUP

M r. Graber was murdered while we were on our way to my parents. And just as Mr. Ayres said in his deteriorated mental state, there were sounds of soup. He was walking Bascombe, as he had been when we saw him earlier that night, talking through the metrics of some sort of rollout for his company involving Motorola radios. It's funny how that has stuck within my memory, as it means nothing to me at all. Just something I heard my neighbor say moments before his death. We were unable to warn him. Such a terrible and helpless feeling, compromising another's ability to flee out of fear for your own survival. Bascombe survived, rushing away from the monstrous attack, into the darkness. And though I would have fallen into the category of people who said things such as, *It always bothers me more when an animal dies in a movie, whereas people hardly bother me much at all*, when it comes to real life, it's equally terrible.

Mr. Graber was considering an option involving SMR licensing as he and Bascombe passed the Clephanes' house and out of view. That's when the light hit him and the night was enriched in shadows. They worked feverishly, pulling Mr. Graber apart. When he hit the street and sidewalk, it was all at once, sloppily spreading with hardly a scream to enunciate his terror. My hope was that he never saw it coming, and the shock and immediacy was so all-encompassing that his mind was unable to register what was happening. Or the blindness of fear blotted out any type of recognition, no sense whatsoever that he was dying in a way that could only be described as reprehensible. And then Bascombe was booking it back into view, crying out and scared, but alive. Exchanging the light for the safety of the darkness. Rushing up the street and behind the Gurneys' house.

Caroline and I sat in the woods, both collapsed by the trauma of reality, sobbing. Covering our mouths to prevent ourselves from vomiting or emoting any sounds that might allow Tarkin to pinpoint our location. Her leaning her weight against a thin tree, head hanging in sad defeat, while I lay face down in the brush, leaves and branches beneath my chest and belly. Tears of such varying degree that they didn't simply leak from the ducts of our eyes but instead spread out across the gutters of our eyelids and overflowed in the ways of a heavy rain. She nudged me after a few minutes, saying it was best we keep moving. We stuck to the woods as our guts insisted and stepped slowly, doing our best not to break branches or shuffle leaves. We found it somewhat horrifying how many households seemed to have no clue as to what was taking place. That same family watching the movie earlier in the night, cuddled safely upon the couch, was now up in the bathroom window brushing their teeth by candlelight. While below, Adam Tarkin walked past staring up at them as though weighing the pros and cons of taking their lives. It was eerie each time we lost sight of him as we made our way behind the houses, taking an inordinate amount of time. Not wanting to leave the safety of the woods, following along the perimeter of Stover Road and down to the bottom of the neighborhood where my house sat.

As was the case earlier, Grandma Dar was back on her feet, wandering around the living room. Every once in a while bringing her small, arthritic hand up to negate the reflection of the candlelight so that she could see out the window.

"She's at it again," Caroline said. "You think she's waiting on someone? I mean, in her mind. Like maybe she used to do that when your mom was young and out after dark, playing with friends or somethin'?"

"That's a sweet thought, but I'm not sure."

And I wasn't. I wasn't sure if it was habit from the time of my mom's youth or perhaps her own. But it made me think of all those times she and my mom spoke when they thought I was in bed or watching TV. Particularly the story about the last time Grandma Dar had seen her daddy alive. Said he was sitting on a porch rocker with a shotgun in his lap as she walked away from the house. She knew without looking back that the blast was him taking himself out of this world. Sheriff Primrose used a scrub brush with an extended handle to erase the violence from the ceiling of the front porch, but it made no matter. She said the stain wouldn't go away. Even after a family friend applied fresh paint, the sadness would somehow seep through. But it was the way she talked about the local mortician and his apprentice collecting pieces of her daddy from the blast that really got me. "Twenty feet from the house," was how she put it, watching from her bedroom window. "They were still pickin' up pieces of Daddy." And it made me wonder if she maybe stood by the window like that as a girl, peeking out and waiting for her father to finish up his work on the farm and come tuck her in at night. It made my heart ache.

My mom lay behind her on the couch, which was not uncommon, what with Grandma Dar's constant wandering at night. No less than three nights a week, she or my dad would lay on the couch to ensure she didn't leave the house or take to the basement steps unaccompanied. Equipped with a thick blanket and pillow, my mom lay with one leg outside the blanket to regulate temperature. With her right arm, she was doing that thing that kids often do, for no apparent reason other than it just kind of feels good, where they put an arm straight up in the air and hold it there. She didn't look at my grandma, but it was apparent she was talking to her by the way her jaw was moving. Likely speaking to her as she often did about when she was a little girl. It was pretty wholesome hearing about my mom's childhood. She and Grandma Dar used to go into the houses of the neighborhood as they were being built. Said they would say a prayer for each family by walking through the skeletal frames of each home. "It was pretty cool," she once told me. "Gram and I would bring flashlights and go in at night and pray. The way the house was framed, it was like walking through a giant skeleton and blessing it from within. Loved the way the fresh wood smelled." Said the wood was like the bones of the house while the electrical outlets and wiring played the part of the nervous system. And then came the drywall and paint, closing it all inside under a protective layer of skin. I always found it neat to look at it that way. Claimed our house was the first in the neighborhood, so they were able to carry out their sweet little ritual in nearly every home.

"I'll go first," I told Caroline. "I'll get my mom to open the door and then you can follow."

Caroline nodded, knowing there was something to the safety of the woods. But our plan would be thrown when Adam Tarkin walked across the street from the Gleasons' yard. We barely saw him until he was about twenty feet from us, but he didn't pay any attention to our whereabouts, even though we were less camouflaged than we'd been most of the way to my parents. His focus was clearly on my house, and in particular, Grandma Dar who still looked out the window with one rheumatic hand shading her view. The other began to move in a sort of spastic way. Sort of way a toddler might move to indicate something exciting was about to happen. My heart beat out of my chest, and I went to call out, but nothing would come. Caroline pulled me from my feet back down into a crouched position and insisted we stay quiet by looking me directly in the eyes and bringing a single finger to her lips. Tarkin was moving at a clip, though still remotely calm, that flashlight at his side with no indication he was about to use it. Then he was flush against the window, Grandma

Dar and him with their foreheads touching glass on either side. Mirroring each other's actions by bringing the palm of each hand against the glass as well. It nearly broke my heart to see Grandma Dar's gnarled little hands go against the window. Tarkin placing his hands in the same manner, as if, had the glass not been between them, their fingers might have intertwined, as innocently as Caroline and I's had earlier that night.

Something innate and ancient took hold, and I hardly remembered making the decision, but all of a sudden, I was chucking a rock I'd located in the dirt at Tarkin. It hit him in the mid-upper back and the human side of him caused his shoulders to come up and hold in a sort of shrug. It broke his trance, and that's when I noticed that I was out in the yard and away from the protection of the woods. Caroline was out too, with both her hands clamped upon my wrist like someone holding a baseball bat, leaning her subtle frame back toward the woods in an attempt to pull me. But by the time I realized this and turned, the lack of weight threw her off balance and caused her to fall down onto her lower back. The light clicked on, and as I went to pull her up from the grass, I saw the shadow of a goat take shape, its horns cutting back across the top of its head, ears just below. Eyes seeming to zero in on Caroline, with a coarse tuft of hair moving upon it's chin as it went to strike. Caroline arched her head away, deflecting the attack. She brought a hand up, as blood leaked between her fingers and immediately ran down the length of her arm where it pooled and dripped from her elbow. And then she was up, and we landed in a heap in the woods as the light clicked out.

"Okay. Okay. You're fine. It's fine," I said, pulling my t-shirt up over my head and applying pressure to the wound. The bite was relinquished to that of the shadowy goat's front teeth, chomping a piece of earlobe and cutting her along the jawline. After that, things went to shit and fervor. Time went in and out like an accordion. I remember my dad at the front door and then down in the grass with us, rushing Caroline into the house as my mom did the same with me. Both out in the yard. And Adam Tarkin was back at the window with Grandma Dar, seemingly locked in place as though the two were stuck on each side like those frogs with the sticky legs. Neither budging, no matter the chaos going on just ten feet away. And I could have sworn as I glanced over that my grandma winked, almost indicating that she would hold him while we got to safety. But when we got in the house, her movements were back to being locked to that window, forehead to forehead, hand to hand, with Adam Tarkin.

"You're alright, sweetheart," my mom told Caroline, directing that I go into the kitchen pantry to get sterile wrap and gauze. She then placed the gauze in the area where Caroline's wounds were and asked that I apply pressure. Blood was soaking through the gauze, but my mother worked to bring the bandage beneath Caroline's chin and up over the top of her head, over and over until the wrap held in place. I sat on the couch with my arm around Caroline as she cried. She'd been strong all night, strong when most of us had wavered, but she was losing it then. She'd come unstrung.

My dad walked up to Grandma Dar carefully as though he was trying not to provoke an aggressive animal and slowly brought the curtains to a close on either side of her until all that was between them was my grandma's tiny little head. Then he took her by the shoulders and slowly guided her away from the window. Tarkin looked up in that moment, staring at my dad and returning to the lifeless shell of a person he'd been earlier that night. And then the curtain fell into place and blocked him where he stood outside. My dad walked Grandma Dar back to the recliner and sat her down, using the switch to get her legs up. She held the expression of a child, making eye contact with my dad and registering an inquisitive smile. And then he was back over with us, crouching, like a player in a game awaiting a call from his coach.

"What happened, baby?" my mom asked.

I began rattling off everything I could remember, telling them about Adam escaping through his bedroom window and what he'd done to Dufour and Bently. And Mr. Ayres and the rest of the neighbors and that poor cop, and when I got to Kemper it was too much to bear. All I could do was say his name, choke it out. My oldest friend. I couldn't tell them what he'd done to Kemper. Not Kemper. That was just something I couldn't manage. She held me like she used to when I was a little boy, clutched to her chest. There was no end to the sadness, fear, and pain. Not even a mother's touch, my mother's touch, could douse those flames.

"It's okay, son. It's gonna be okay. And you too, young lady. You are both safe now," my dad said. But we weren't. He hadn't a clue of what was to come. There was no safety from a beast of such misfortune. There seemed no end to the darkness we found ourselves in. And then there were shadows. Along the wall behind us, working into shapes. Caroline and I slid from the couch, down onto the carpet and hugged each other tightly. But my parents weren't afraid. They simply rubbed our backs and comforted us like upset children. Grandma Dar's arthritic knuckles popped and locked in place, causing the shadows to do the same. She mumbled, as I'd heard her mumble so many times before, about her daddy. But this was the first time she shared this particular memory. How he used to come in from the fields and lay with her, set a candle upon her bedside table, and make wonderful shapes upon the wall. Shapes that told a story. Shapes that brought to life an entire world. One beyond anything she'd ever imagined. She'd always spoken of her daddy so lovingly, as though the tragic events of his death could not outweigh the life he'd lived up until that point. My mom said it was due to him having a stroke and losing the ability to provide for his family. Said it was a shame he was unable to bear. She never knew that I heard about the way he died, but I guess she assumed I'd heard enough to put two and two together. He'd apparently lost the ability to use most of his left side, dragging it along with him, trying to work the fields to no avail.

"It's happening the way she feared it would," my mom said.

"Mom," I asked, "what are you talking about?"

"Amy?" my dad also asked.

My mom told us a story that we'd heard before, at least to some extent. One of Grandma Dar and Grandpa Dean moving into the very house we were standing in, but the events leading up to it were something we'd never known. She reiterated how she and Grandma Dar used to walk through the homes, blessing them and praying for the families that would one day live inside, though this time she told us why they found that necessary. When I'd first heard such stories, I thought it nothing more than presenting good faith toward new neighbors, as their Catholic upbringings might teach, but this went beyond that.

"This land was thought to be burdened, which I know sounds absolutely ridiculous. In fact, that's how I always kind of thought of it. As some sort of old wives' tale, but there were people who believed."

"I don't understand," my dad said. "What are you talking about?"

"This land once belonged to Grandma and her family and had been passed down through generations. It was Great-Grandpa Jeffrey's pride and joy, owning one of the most bountiful farms in all of Upper Hearth. Still worked it with his wife and your grandma and some of the nieces and nephews on the Ampler side of the family until he became too sick. But that's not what did him in. It wasn't the stroke, but rather the folks trying to take the land for their own gain. The sadness of family betrayal. There was an uncle by the name of Neeman, one your grandma had only met on occasion, who'd offered a buyout, but Great-Grandpa Jeffrey wouldn't budge. He had a mind to pass the farm on to Grandma Dar and her children. It all went south when he had that stroke."

"What does this have to do with anything?" my dad asked, but I knew the moment she'd said the name Jeffrey.

"Uncle Neeman was able to convince most of the family not to help out on the farm after Great-Grandpa Jeffrey passed away. Promised them this and that, and eventually your great-grandma was forced to sell to him. It wasn't long after that that the fruit started rotting. Came up out of the ground or grew from the vine looking flawless, but inside was nothing but rot." She said that was only the beginning though. Uncle Neeman and his family suffered loss after terrible loss. First, their oldest son died when his tractor overturned. Then the youngest daughter drowned in the swimming hole that once ran from the creek. And it was his wife, Maive, that finally spooked him into selling. Claimed to have seen his brother walking the property at night. Said he'd spoken to her, told her that he'd never let them live in peace. That the rot was coming for them as well. And showed her terrible images of their children rotting in the ground, as though some sort of dream. Said he pulled back the grass and dirt at his feet and showed her the two of them in different stages of decomposition and that they too told her to leave. Said that if they didn't, she'd have to lay down beside them. Not long after that, he sold to a man by the name of Marmol who ran a mink farm down in Lower Guild. Talked of bringing the project to Upper Hearth where the ground wasn't always sopping and soft. He thought it'd be an easier work environment for his people. But those mink escaped one night. Same night, a fire broke out and killed Marmol and his wife. "After that, no one showed interest in this property for nearly twenty years until JP Pageant bought the property with an aim to build this neighborhood. But he took a different approach. Growing up in the area and hearing the stories, he offered Grandma Dar the very first house, free of charge, in hopes that he might lift the misfortune that seemed buried in the land. She'd adopted me, and Grandpa Dean was only making so much delivering mail, so they really had nowhere to go, and so they agreed. Folks were hesitant at first, but stories eventually fade or get downgraded to harmless, and within a few months new construction was going up all around us. Including the house the Tarkins eventually bought. Where the original farmhouse once stood. It was no secret why your grandma asked for the furthest house from that point. The memories were just too much."

"He isn't going anywhere," Grandma Dar said. She no longer worked her crippled fingers before the candle but instead sat back where the shadows played on her features. In my mind I saw her ripping up out of that chair and climbing up the walls like some sort of human spider, casting a pointed finger our way and condemning us. But soon after saying her peace, she seemed to fall asleep. Soft, slow breaths could be heard. Then the faintest little snores.

"Is she asleep?" Caroline asked.

"Odd, right?" my mom followed. "She's like a toddler. Up and at 'em and then two minutes later, sawing logs."

Outside we heard screams. Horrific screams. We rushed over to the window, and Adam Tarkin was working his shadows on Alexander Parm. Parm worked nights at Ventra Freight, running shipments in and out of the country at all hours. We'd see him rushing out to his car to help unload trucks and to ensure customer schedules were met, and my guess would be that his poor timing was what landed him in the clutches of Tarkin. But Grandma saved him. Not on purpose or by any sort of heroics, as her frail little body was of course in no shape for such things, but by simply waking up from the screaming and coming back to that window. She pushed up between my mom and I and once again put her head against the glass, and just that quickly, the light kicked out, and Alexander Parm was beating it back up through the yard and into his house. Something was clearly wrong with his left arm, as it sort of dangled, dislodged, bouncing to the metrics of his rushing legs, but he was alive. And not many who'd come face to face with Tarkin would be able to say as much.

Adam turned on a dime, with absolute precision, doing something similar to an about-face a soldier might showcase in military formation. Walking back up through our lawn and to the window where Grandma stood. Only this time, he started working his hands at the bottom of the window, trying to raise it up so he could get inside. And when this didn't work, we found him walking with purpose to the front door where the handle danced dangerously back and forth, and the hinges threatened to come out from the frame.

"*Dad,*" I cried out.

And though I can't recall what was said, we worked to get the sofa moved to the front hallway, wedging it between the front door and the railing of the staircase which came down just to the side of the front door, as many houses did in those days. There was no pounding or frustration on Tarkin's part; he simply was trying to get inside to Grandma Dar. But we weren't sure of his intentions. She started telling us, "*Daddy wants in. That's all. Daddy wants to see me.*" She said this with the disdain of a child being told no, simply speaking about her dad. Asking that we let him in. Wanting to be in his presence.

"Mom," my mom said, "why don't we go sit down. Just take it easy."

Tarkin was once again at the window, peering in between the curtains as my dad drew them closed. There was familiarity in his eyes, almost human again, but not the boy I'd known. The familiarity was something else altogether. Something that belonged to whatever it was that had taken him over.

My mother sat Grandma down and immediately went upstairs where her movements could be heard through the ceiling. Caroline was looking at me with the saddest expression I'd ever known. Something that, in those moments, made me believe she wished she'd never met me. Never come to this godforsaken neighborhood with Julie to simply hang out and have a good time. And that bothered me. It made me sick to think that never knowing me was an acceptable alternative. And it also pissed me off that we were suffering such sick, sad violence at such an early age. I felt then, and feel now, that no child should ever suffer through such things. Our teenage years had been swallowed whole. Gobbled up by torturous sadness.

When my mother returned, she motioned that I should come sit with Grandma Dar and pull up a chair from the kitchen. Adam remained in the window; eyes locked on her and nothing else. She sat an old photo album in Grandma's lap. The leather sloughed away from it like flakes of dead skin. She opened the first page to reveal a toddler in a pretty white dress, sitting in freshly cut grass. The picture was that faded, old-timey type, where it looked jaundiced or yellowed by nicotine.

"That's you, Mom," my mom said to her. "Remember?"

And that's when it became clear what we needed to do. Caroline walked over and drug a kitchen chair behind her, unaware or uncaring of the way its back legs scraped across the kitchen floor and into the living room where we sat. Earlier in the night, she'd done much the same, dragging a chair across the house to block the garage door over at Kemper's, and now she brought one over to where Grandma Dar and I sat to open a door of memories. My mom and dad walked into the kitchen and talked in hushed tones as Caroline and I flipped through the pages of the album, asking Grandma questions about who was in the pictures or when they were taken. There was one of her on an old tractor with Rumley Oil Pull written in swooping letters on the front box where the auxiliary exhaust came out from the cylinder. She couldn't have been more than seven or eight and looked so tiny sitting up in the seat. And the man who stood alongside her, in the old hat, seemed so proud, holding her in place and looking toward the camera. In my mind I could almost picture the man coaxing her to look toward the camera. But he wasn't smiling. It always seemed that the men and women in those times were not made to smile the way subsequent generations were made to. This picture was no different.

"Daddy's tractor," Grandma Dar told us, moving an arthritic paw upon the page and allowing her crooked little pointer to direct us to the tractor. "Daddy," she said, moving ever so slightly to cover the man's face. And it was at that point that I looked up to see the very same man peering through the front window. Only the left side of his face didn't seem to cooperate with the features of his right. Whereas the right held a slight grin and thick, furrowed brow, the left simply drooped in the fashion of a slightly filled water balloon. Caroline saw him too, the exact same face that I was seeing, Calm Jeffrey. I knew this by the way she took my arm around the bicep and sort of pulled it toward her. And then we both saw Adam Tarkin again, forehead against the glass, to the point where his hair splayed away where he was making contact.

"There's also this," my mom said, carrying an old hardback ledger. She sat it before us and Caroline immediately began rummaging through it. The penmanship was perfection, written with great care, and the words were none other than my grandmother's, though clearly written in the infancy of her life. "I haven't looked at it in years. Honestly, kind of forgot it even existed."

"*August 16th, 1943,*" Caroline began to read. "*Daddy worked the cattle today. Most of them bound for slaughter, but a few that needed hoof trimming to remove dirt and gravel and inspect for parasites. He was tired. Clearly tired, as his work knows no bounds. Even still, he found it within him to wash up and lay beside me before bed and ask questions about my day. I told him about Patrick Kearny making fun of my forehead. He laughed and assured me that my forehead was among the finest in all of Upper Hearth before planting a loving kiss upon it. And somehow that made me feel better. Didn't completely alleviate my insecurities, but in a way, relinquished them to background noise. He brought me a gift but told me that I was to wait until morning, which was to be on a Saturday, before pursuing my desires to read it. It was a beautiful leatherbound copy of Emily Bronte's "Wuthering Heights". As I was her biggest fan and had a mind to write such lovely words one day, I begged that he at least let me keep it upon my bedside table where I might stare at it until sleep had its way. Even now, as I write these words, I long to put them together in such a way that would make Emily proud. And before leaving, he shared his gift with me. Taking the plated candle and bedside table and aligning them before him where he sat at the bottom of my bed crisscross applesauce. Such strange witness was it to see a man of my father's age and masculinity sit that way after tending to the fields of exhaustion. And that's what he called them. The fields of exhaustion. What a term. Really, that was literally something Emily may have put down upon the page. "His hands were magic. I watched them, unable to reason his ability to contort them into such exquisite and lovely shapes. There was the bird flying up into the sky, its beak moving to the metrics of Daddy's puckered, whistling lips. And of course, the elephant, of which I'd only seen in picture books from the library. But my most favorite was the man in the hat. Daddy said it was him, though he only wore a hat in the fields and on occasion when running into town. But the man was so funny. He spoke in Daddy's voice. Telling stories from before I was born or when Daddy was little. I did my best not to watch Daddy's mouth moving out of the corner of my eye and instead believe that his shadowy-self was alive and reeling through tales from the past. And sometimes he told me stories of the future, such as this night. Told stories of my future husband and I taking over the farm and raising a family and living a beautiful life. And then, just as my eyes became weary and the story was coming to a close, I'd feel that same soft kiss upon the forehead Patrick Kearny mocked and a wisp of breath as my father whispered goodnight and blew out the candle."*

I sat perplexed by what Caroline had shared, unable to come to terms between what I'd witnessed and what she was saying. It all lined up. The shadows on Tarkin's wall growing up. The elephant. The man in the old hat. Calm Jeffrey. Great-grandfather, purveyor of nightmares and horrible reality. Trumner's great-uncle was one of the engineers who designed the Lincoln Continental JFK was assassinated in. Funny, the dude was failing history but could tell you all about how Ford Motor Company originally assembled the Lincoln but then handed it over to Hess and Eisenhardt for the custom build where they went about extending the overall length, added *the* jump seat, and customized an interchangeable roof that could be reduced to a convertible. Seemed like I was getting the short end of it all, what with his uncle building the Lincoln JFK was assassinated in and my great-grandfather being responsible for the murder of several of our friends and neighbors. Whole thing seemed kind of fucked if I'm to be honest. And I know that sounds petty. In hindsight, I'm sort of embarrassed to even admit it, but it definitely crossed my mind.

She skimmed through the ledger, using a finger to quickly read through passages. Her eyes were so beautifully focused that I'd nearly forgotten not twenty minutes prior her ear had nearly been ripped from its place and discarded in our front lawn. Something I found to be both sickening and unfathomable. She did this thing where she bit down on her bottom lip when hyper focused. It's something she continues to do to this day, and I dare not tell her for fear that she might become aware and stop. Such a strange thought, that you can manipulate another's actions by simply pointing out said actions, but it happens all the time. And I'm just not about that.

"*Here*," Caroline said. My mom and dad came into the room and parked their asses on the coffee table. Grandma Dar was surprisingly alert as well, clearly unaware that anything she was hearing had been written by her own hand. She leaned forward a bit, causing the photo album to slide from her lap where I was forced to sort of pin it between my knee and the recliner to stop its fall. Such an eerie feeling, collecting it to a picture of Great-Grandpa Jeffrey wearing denim overalls with the front pocket torn and hanging like a bunny ear. A rolled cigarette clinging to the corner of his mouth. But his eyes were friendly. Optimistic even. And his shoulders and chest strong beneath the cotton of his shirt. As though this photo tapped into his comfort zone where life was on par with what he'd imagined. And I guess that's when things feel disastrous, when they veer from what we imagined. As though we have any control over such cataclysmic plans. And that's why John Lennon said that thing so many years ago. The one I'd read in a *Rolling Stone* or some other magazine about pain being the state we spend most of our time in. And how soft we must be, to feel pain when plans play out the way they're supposed to, against our will and waning desire for control. But I had to admit, the past several hours had been painful. Worst kind I'd ever known. And irrevocably violent, and I was more than unhappy about nearly all of it. But not everything.

Caroline shared a passage of the day Great-Grandpa Jeffrey collapsed in the fields. Her mother came running toward the house in a panic unlike anything she'd witnessed. "*Mama was breathing at a clip likened to when we play in the school yard. Type of breath that inhibits all ability to speak, but she had no mind to speak anyhow. Instead, she went right to the farm bell and sent out a message of distress. Ringing the bell three times, followed by a brief pause before two final rings. A code my father had instilled in the both of us to sound the alarm to neighboring farms of an emergency. Willis Coover and his son Peak were the first to respond, and Mama hopped in the truck to head them off on the drive. They spoke between vehicles in frantic tones of which I could not make out from the porch, but I knew that Mama was on her way to get help."* She went on to talk about a Packard Henney pulling into the gravel drive just as Willis and Peak brought her daddy out from the fields in the back of their truck. Only, instead of Willis driving as he was before, Peak then drove as Willis tended to her daddy. *"After that, Daddy just wasn't right. In fact, the left side of his body was to blame. It no longer functioned with the capabilities it once offered. Instead, the arm hung limp and loose as the strings of a Chinese hand drum. And his foot drug behind and provided less stability than required to support Daddy's body. But he still tried to work. Still tried to be the man he once was. But life will have its way with you. His speech was slaughtered, coming out slow and monotone, and his facial response was mostly void of emotion. In a matter of months, all spirit had left him. Sure, he'd gained back a portion of his physical strength, but his sadness was on the front of our minds. And he and Mama spoke quietly about losing the farm."*

"You said, a few months back, when the incident happened at school, Mrs. Tarkin went out and rang that bell, right?" Caroline asked.

"I guess," I agreed. "To some degree. I can't say there was a pattern. Neighbors said she went out and rang it frantically. Clearly in a bad place. Not sure if she received a call from the school or what, but definitely odd behavior."

"And that was how many months ago?"

"Two? Maybe three?" I told her.

"It was mid-August," my mom said. "I remember coordinating with the neighbors to bring them dinner." Now, I'd never been much further than Chicago at that point and can't say this is a common thing outside of the south, but when a neighbor is in a bad way, it's near certain the troops will rally. At least initially, until the excitement of one's tragedy wanes and is quietly reverted back to those suffering. It's the whole out of sight, out of mind thing. After that, it's all the humdrum of normalcy and people go back to their lives. But there is at least a momentary concerted effort to assist those in need. An effort to take away the basic concern of *What are we gonna have for dinner tonight?*

"What are you getting at?" my dad asked.

"She rang that bell earlier tonight. Some sort of pattern that was clear communication between her and Adam."

"It's true. He did come home. Briefly. Just before..." but I couldn't finish. Didn't want to. Images of Kemper crept back into my mind, and I felt like I might be sick. Imagined the terror on his face as his body was stretched beyond its limitations. A look of severity and desperation. Type of desperation one registers when unbearable violence plays upon them.

Caroline pointed to the date of the entry she just read, and she and my mom both agreed the incident with Adam Tarkin at school could have taken place on the same day, approximately fifty years later.

"What's today's date?" Caroline asked, rummaging through the pages of the ledger.

"November third" my dad said.

"No," my mom corrected him. "Today's the fifth."

"It is. That's right. My fault. It's the fifth."

Caroline located what she was searching for and again began reading from the ledger. "*November 12th, 1943. Nearly a week has passed since the tragedy that befell my family. And still I find it nearly impossible to put into words, though my mindset is to do it now, while the facts are fresh and skewed by nothing more than utter shock and sadness. But not time. Time has a way of distorting facts. So, my hope is to at least avoid that mistake. On the last evening, I was to stay on our family farm. Daddy was out in the fields for an inordinate amount of time. My mother rang the bell on numerous occasions out of fear, and he hollered back that he would be home in due time. It was shortly following sundown that we would hear the animals. It could not be known in that time as to what was happening, but from the bitter comments of Uncle Neeman, I have learned that each was led from pasture unknowingly to their deaths. My suspicion, though it is nothing I care to speak, is that my daddy, being in his broken state, had a mind to ensure no scavenger pursuing ownership of the farm would have success. Though their fate was brutal, falling from the high cliff on the west side of our property, little could be heard from where my mama and I stayed at the house. Shadows could be seen from Daddy's lantern as he walked to retrieve each animal, one by one, in a sort of ritualistic fashion. And at least some small part of me believes this was done out of love. I know that sounds strange, but it felt as though Daddy's whole aim was to take them to a better place. One void of the cruel and selfish ways of this world. A subject that Daddy spoke of at tedium the last few months. When he finally came to the house, his body was near collapse. Sweat bleached his skin and clothing, and there seemed little strength available to get him inside. Mama went to him where he stood, taking his face in her hands and placing her forehead against his until he pushed her aside and walked through the front door. He sat down at the kitchen table where Mama rewarmed stew and beans and the necessities to rebuild his strength. He no longer wished to eat in our presence. Embarrassed. His mouth unable to hold a proper bite. Much of what he ate fell back to the bowl where he would have another go of it. So, Mama and I waited before the fire for him to finish. As sad as it had become to listen to my daddy speak, there was still a portion of me that cherished his stories at the end of an evening. And that evening, being at the end of the week and followed by no school, my mama was more likely to allow that I stay up. But there was a different feeling on that night. One of finality, and I believe she sensed it. She insisted I be off to bed. I did so, hesitantly, going to the table to place a kiss upon Daddy's forehead before telling him goodnight. And that was, to the best of my knowledge, the only time in my life that he was too disenchanted to respond. Instead, setting his spoon alongside his bowl and staring out at nothing."*

What happened next came down to a matter of inches. That was all that was necessary. Grandma Dar suddenly hyper aware, once again pointing a shaky, malformed finger toward the window. Caroline's eyes widening as she clung to the ledger. And that's when I remembered how Tarkin broke it all down. Explaining the nuances to Kemper and I. Same way he did that night in his bedroom, bringing his hands toward the flashlight. "See, the closer you are, the less the light's able to spread." We watched from our sleeping bags, elbows propping our heads, as he cast an enormous, blurry rabbit upon his bedroom wall. "Whereas the further you get from the light, the more distinct the features. It's sort of like when Mrs. Fromeyer adjusts the focus on the projector," showing how the shadowy rabbit shrank in size as he brought his hands away. And it was this technique that Tarkin implemented as two shadowy hands slowly parted the drapes of the front window. After all we'd done to barricade the entryways, we failed that most basic necessity. Leaving the curtains a quarter of an inch open. Full on darkness followed, one enormous hand collecting us like a child's playthings. So intelligent was its strength, constricting and relinquishing its grip based on our contorted efforts of escape. Visibility was nonexistent and our ability to speak was eliminated by pressure. Sort you feel when someone squeezes you in a bearhug or walks on your back causing you to hold your breath and tighten your abdomen.

Then came sounds of furniture being rearranged and the bolt of the front door rescinding into its hardware. An eerie silence fell upon us. My mom went to speak, and our world tightened once again. Bulging our eyes. Knocking the wind from our bellies. Our little planet of pain. And then the creak of the front door swinging wide, followed by a momentary pause before shuffling feet could be heard upon the hardwood. She was all alone. I knew that much. Grandma Dar was not a part of what we suffered. Likely still seated in that recliner as vulnerable as a baby bird. She mumbled about Daddy, but that was all I could understand. One thing was certain, though; the ghosts of the past were upon her. Serving up omissions of contaminated reality. The ones most find implausible, intolerable, or religiously blasphemous.

It was wicked and unnecessary, what the shadow inflicted upon my dad, dragging him by the ankle of his left foot with such force that he came off raggedy. Without muscle and tendon. Knocking his bones against the walls. The coffee table overturned splintering and impaling him beneath the ribs. He groaned in pain. Mashed his teeth and grimaced. The weight of him seemingly weightless, tossed about the room. A projectile of flesh and bone. And when his right foot was let loose of the shadowy grip, it was clearly on backward, toes in line with his calf, as though God put him together backwards.

Without hesitation, my mom removed the wood where it stuck in his side. He was unconscious by then. Limp. Blood surfaced like oil. She placed a palm of pressure against the wound. We'd later learn he was penetrated between his false ribs just below the left lung, avoiding collapse. Ensuring my mom only need to focus on stopping the bleeding and not deal with any other catastrophes. I ran up the steps and grabbed bath towels. My mom counting down. Removing her hand and allowing that I pack the wound with one of the towels before reapplying pressure. She insisted I call for help, but that was simply panic talking. Stark reality quickly set us straight. No one was coming. We were all on our own. And that's when my mom's panic hit another level. *"Where's Mom?"* she screamed, looking around the room frantically. *"Where's your grandmother?"* I turned and looked about the room, automatically walking to the recliner where she was last seen and then over to the open front door of our house.

"I know where she is," Caroline said, sitting in the corner of the room, paging through the ledger.

FIELDS OF EXHAUSTION

Walt and Lita Jennings were at their front door, shining a flashlight our way. They were an older couple, not Grandma's age by any means, but ancient in that way anyone over sixty seems to a teenager. Walt was a grumpy fellow, and his wife was sweet to a degree of annoyance. When I was younger, there wasn't a time my mom and I walked by without her coming out to hand me a popsicle on a hot day, or fruit snacks that always seemed slightly melted from the way she waited by the window and held them in her hand. Honestly, I think she was just kind of lonely. They had a daughter who moved away and that seemed to be the extent of their livelihood. Mrs. Jennings always offered us things she'd kept from when her daughter was little. My first tricycle had a tiny license plate that swung down from the seat which simply read, *LISA.*

"*Robbie Bausch*?" Walt hollered.

My dad sold them car insurance when I was little, and I recalled sitting in their kitchen while he ran through the paperwork. Conservative talk radio played on the radio, and though it was early in the day, a litany of empty Budweiser cans sat on the sink where they had been rinsed and set to dry. I remember getting my dad to crack up later that day by asking if Republicans recycled. My dad was surprised by my knowledge of the two-party system in our county. One that Miss Canty so lopsidedly taught us about in fifth grade. He explained to me that most people had more in common than not, and that everyone was just doing what they thought to be the proper thing. It was during that time that I realized my dad was simply one of the few people I'd ever meet that truly just wanted people to get along.

"Wait here," I told Caroline. Though we needed to move quickly, there was still a necessity to stay near the woods. Where the property from the old farm ended. So, going out to talk to the Jennings was not without its risks. "Be right back."

As I walked up to Walt and Lita Jennings, they lowered the beam of light down upon the bottom half of my body. Even that little bit of light shining upon me got my heart racing again. Made me think of those images upon the side of the Miosis' house. The ones that took our friends away.

"Good evening, Mr. and Mrs. Jennings," I began.

"That *is* Robbie?" Lita began. "*Oh, look how grown up you're getting.*"

"We're just taking a little walk is all. Trying to make our way up to the front of the neighborhood to see when the power will be back on. You all should just try and get some rest. I'm sure things will be up and running by morning."

"Looks a little strange," Walt said. "What with you creepin' through the neighbors' yards and all."

"Oh, she enjoys it."

"Who?" Lita asked.

"Oh, my girlfriend. We were just jokin' around."

"*Girlfriend?*" she said, louder than I would have preferred. Inciting embarrassment, even during such circumstances. "*Oh, Robbie's got himself a girlfriend.*" Making a big deal of it, waving across the street where Caroline, caught off guard, began to wave back.

"Huh," Walt more grunted. "Is that right?"

"We were just reminiscing how we used to sneak out when we were little is all."

And that was the end of it. They sent me on my way as the front door closed, and the deadbolt was thrown. No harm, no foul. It felt odd that I was in a place where I waited and listened to ensure the door was locked behind them before feeling comfortable enough to walk away from their house.

We spent several seconds alongside the Penningtons' house before deciding it was clear enough to move on. And that's how we operated, with the woods behind us, should we need to retreat. Assessing the safety of our movements, house by house. At one point, we heard Bascombe and fled to the woods. The high-pitched, nasally whine taking us off guard and causing an impulse of panic. And though we quickly realized where it was coming from, we didn't dare shine our light. Through the darkness we could make out the sad situation the canine was in, watching as Bascombe lay across the lower torso of Mr. Graber's body, as though making some sort of futile attempt to pin the man's soul down.

"Poor baby," Caroline said.

We cut behind the Penningtons' and up along the side of the Kaelins' white brick two-story. Caroline pointed out that the white brick would make us more visible, so we made the quick decision to move on to the next house. There was risk, but much more by staying put. "We're like deer in a field," was the way she put it. And it made total sense. When we paused alongside the Vernins' house, she stopped dead in her tracks. I was already peering around the corner and determining our next move when she asked, "Can we check on them?" The house was the same one I told her about earlier, vacant of a father. In the window was the mother, peering out to try and get a handle on what might be going on. Caroline stepped out into the front yard, and I automatically joined her. This seemed personal; something she simply had to do. As we neared the house, we saw the woman step away from the front window and allow the curtains to fall back in place. There was no need to knock. We could hear, almost feel her movements coming to greet us at the door. When she opened it, she was white as a ghost, almost translucent, framed by the inner darkness of the house.

"Can we go with you?" she asked.

"It's not safe," Caroline told her. "But we'll bring help, okay? Just sit tight. Keep your entryways blocked, and no matter how much you want to, don't look outside."

"The Tarkin boy," she said. "The kids heard strange sounds outside the window."

It was then that we realized they'd witnessed the death of Mr. Graber, or at the very least, its aftermath. She began shaking at an unsustainable rate. Her own personal earthquake. We turned around to find Adam Tarkin standing on the sidewalk. Staring past us. At the house. As though we were merely an appetizer. Upstairs, the children peeked out the window with innocent, frightened faces. The light clicked upon them. And that's when we saw Mickey Watts tiptoeing quickly across the street, coming toward Tarkin. Mickey was sort of a high school phenom due to a scholarship he'd landed playing baseball at Cal State Fullerton under Augie Garrido, though he ended up tearing both his MCL and ACL and those days went out the window only three weeks into his freshman season. Since then, he mostly worked at the gas station off Bernie Road and drank in his parents' basement. Became a bit of a recluse. That was, until making the decision to high-step it across the street and crack Adam Tarkin across the back of the head with an aluminum baseball bat. It was an odd moment, nearly slapstick the way the bat made that hollow *ping* I'd heard so many times as a child playing knothole. Tarkin went down lifelessly upon the sidewalk.

The woman slapped the door shut behind us, and we were once again greeted by the all too familiar sound of a deadbolt being thrown. Mickey stood over Tarkin, looking down at him in the same manner we'd seen in all those '80s horror movies growing up. Right before the killer came back to life only to execute the person by way of overzealous and often banal violence. Blood quickly spread out beneath Tarkin's head. Filling the cracks and crevices of the sidewalk. Pooling. And for a split second, I saw Adam Tarkin for what he was. A kid. Just a kid. A year younger than me, actually. He was just so damned smart. But Caroline knew the calm was momentary and pulled me by my arm.

"*Come on,*" she insisted. "*We need to leave.*"

As we began to turn and run, that light clicked on again. Dark shadows encased Mickey to the point that only his feet, neck, and head could be seen. Reminded me of Elmyra Duff's suffocating love, squeezing animals in those old cartoons, causing their insides to be cast down into their nether regions or up into their ballooning heads. And just as I'd made a decision to turn and get to Tarkin and knock that flashlight free, the way Kemper did for me all those years ago, we heard it. The vomitous eruption of Mickey's insides splattering upon the sidewalk and up onto the woman's front lawn. Mickey's body dropped like a saturated blanket as we ran up the street and through the Ellisons' backyard.

We gave a wide berth when running around the front of the house, aware of the destruction we'd heard play out earlier that evening. What drew my attention first was the way several neighbors seemingly remained seated in their collapsible chairs. Nancy Darwick's mammoth body sat beside her husband, Orin. Only Nancy's head was nowhere in the vicinity. Judging from what we'd witnessed earlier, there was a chance it was across the street or down in the woods behind the Tarkins'. There was no telling what played out during those moments. Orin was mostly intact, other than the area where his right leg had been torn from the socket of his hip. Unlike his wife's missing portions, his leg was discarded down near the curb where we once popped tar bubbles on hot summer days.

What stayed with me though, and stands out in my mind to this day, was seeing Mr. Ellison's slip-on laying in the middle of the sidewalk. It seems so silly to say, but there was just something sad about it. Or maybe it was my way of deflecting from the carnage all around us and giving it a centralized location in that overgrown man's footwear. It wasn't like his severed foot was still planted inside, with bone bright as ivory coming out from a portion of sock where his shin should have been. Hell, not even sure there was any blood at all, likely because Ellison, as many were that night, was hit with such force that he was literally knocked from his shoes. Even still, there was something that sickened me. Something that solidified that terrible things had taken place. Something final.

She'd read from the ledger before we left the house. As my mom tended to my dad and I sought out dark clothing to camouflage our movements, she sat at the edge of my bed in an overgrown, dark purple hoodie Grandma had gifted my mom for Christmas. And I slipped on a pair of Nike sweatpants and a matching hoodie that I'd never actually worn as a set. Oh, how that drove Grandma crazy, always pointing out how I was not wearing them the way they were intended to be worn. Unable to comprehend that it was not something kids my age did. Shaking her head in disappointment, mumbling that it didn't make any sense. It was while putting on those clothes for the first time as a set that I found myself nauseous with worry.

"My daddy's heart was, without question, built upon the perpetual love of family. That much I want to be known. Even now, orphaned and living without parents, I do not doubt his loyalty and purpose. There was just something broken in his brain is all. Something beyond repair. Not to mention the pressures of being a provider. While my mama tended to my needs and ensured the house stay in order, meals were prepared and I was doing well in school, Daddy worked. And when a man of such independence loses an ability to do so, well, that is detrimental to the soul. Self-worth goes out the window. Sour thoughts are ingested. And I have no doubt that when Daddy stepped away from that table and presented the barrel to the back of Mama's head, he was not thinking about anything more than ending the pain. His current pain and her future pain. And may God forgive me for running, escaping through my bedroom

window after he projected my mama's memories all over the stones of the fireplace, but I just wasn't ready to go with her. Couldn't go with her. And I believe there is a part of me that will always wonder if that was my duty. And as he stepped onto that porch and saw his only daughter hurriedly walking away...had he felt in some way, betrayed."

We sat in the bushes knowing that Mrs. Tarkin's time was numbered. Just as described in the ledger, she was sitting in the front room with her back to us, before the radiant glow of the fireplace. She looked frail. Only the tips of her shoulders and tiny head presented above the back of the sofa. She used to read on that sofa all the time. When we came into the house, there was always a book open and lying face down on the armrest. The one closest to the kitchen. Not sure it was the same author but seemed to be the same guy on all the covers. Thick, chiseled jaw. Long blonde hair highlighted by sun or moonlight. Shirtless, or at the very least, unbuttoned or torn down to his navel. There was even one I remembered with the man's rippling muscles spreading out into angel wings, a woman in a blue dress standing before him, right palm nearly flush against his chest. She actually blushed when we came in by surprise with that one, fumbling to set the book down and changing the subject by asking us about our day.

"How are we gonna get her out?" I asked.

"We're not," Caroline said. "We're gonna get that gun."

And she was right. *I'll be gotdamned*, she was right. Moving a grown woman was plausible, though not easy, but pulling that gun down from where it hung above the fireplace, now that was something we could do.

"You stay here and watch for Tarkin," she said.

"*Wait. What? No way. I'm not letting you go in there.*"

"You have to. Besides, this is the easier of the two tasks."

"How do you mean?"

"I don't want to deal with that fuck," she said, smiling nervously. "Just slow him down, okay?"

"Slow him down?" I said. "How the shit am I supposed to do that?"

Then came the sirens. Our hearts racing. By the sound of them, they were only a few minutes away. I began to stand up until Caroline grabbed my hand and yanked me back down to a crouch. I felt slight relief knowing we would no longer be facing things alone, but the look on her face reminded me that there was not enough time. And when we saw Tarkin walking up the street, she let out for the house without saying a word. There was no change in his mannerisms, and the sirens in the distance seemed to have little effect on his pace. It was as though his timing was always right. That no matter what was happening in the peripheral, each step Adam Tarkin took was in direct correlation with history. Coming in from the fields as the ancient ghost of this land once did. Stepping in unison to the metrics of time.

At a loss for a better idea, I found myself running from my refuge of the front bushes and out across the street. The light was upon me almost immediately, and I felt something trip me up at the ankles, causing me to roll onto my side momentarily in the Ellisons' front yard. I slid through the carnage of internal organs and saturated grass before getting to my feet and popping through the front door. The house smelled of grilled food, as my eyes fought to adjust. I walked up the front hallway with the fingers of my right-hand traipsing along the wall while my left stayed out in front of me to ensure I didn't walk into anything. Moonlight came in through the kitchen window and lit the faux gems of the kitchen counters like a beacon. I began rushing my hands across them in an attempt to locate Mr. Ellison's car keys. In doing so, I knocked what felt to me like a cutting board containing diced onions and tomatoes from the counter where they spilled out onto floor. As my eyes began to adjust, I saw a small desk-like area built beneath a few cabinets. Mounted hooks hung above the desk, but there were no keys. As an act of desperation, I went in that direction anyhow and noted a thin jacket hanging from the back of the chair. I pulled it away at the shoulder and registered that familiar jingle of what I was so desperately looking for. I made my way to the front room and looked out the window to see Caroline carefully stepping up onto the fireplace to retrieve the shotgun. Tarkin was roughly three houses away at that point. Closing in. As Mrs. Tarkin stood and went after Caroline.

You can never fully prepare yourself for what it takes to run a person over, but that's exactly what I intended to do. In the garage, I walked with my hands held high until I found the release latch. The cord hit and I wound it around my palm and back of my hand before pulling that latch loose with a pop. In a motion of pure fury, I went to the garage door and threw it up overhead. It hit with such momentum that it nearly popped back down its tracks, causing me to reach up and try and keep it in place. And then I was behind the wheel, turning the key and clicking on the lights. What a juxtaposition I'd found myself in, to finally light up Tarkin's world. Only, it wasn't Tarkin that I pushed that pedal down on, but rather Scottie Mills the mailman. In his parcel uniform, as he'd been in those days, a bag slung over his shoulder with white envelopes jutting up from the pouch. And as I moved toward him, at a clip I was unaware myself capable, I saw the sadness in his eyes. The same sadness he must have presented the day he was struck and killed. One of unequivocal mourning. For the life he lived and the life he lost. One that assured his daughters would grow up without a father and his wife would love another, slightly less, a few years later. One you never quite prepare yourself for until it comes your way at a significant speed and strikes you with an impact only the dead can understand.

There was the sound of breath leaving his body, Adam Tarkin's body, but in those moments, Scottie Mills the mailman's body. And then he was severed in half. Not by this reality, but the one that took place years ago. The one that pinned him against that guardrail and left his insides to shine in the alternating red and blue lights of first responders. And it didn't stop there. No, instead, that same torso was coming my way like it did in my dreams as a child. As it moved across my bed in that hobgoblin fashion, palms smacking the hood of the car as he neared the windshield.

What sadness it was to awaken moments later, Adam Tarkin laid within the brush of the woods that the car had taken us down into. He looked angelic. Peaceful. As though the demons had been vanquished. There was something wholesome to him again. Just looked like a young man simply sleeping. Eliciting a thought of Kemper saying, *"Tarkin, dude, what are you doing laying out in the woods? Get yer ass up here in a sleeping bag. It's time for eternal rest.*" There was little blood or swelling, and a part of me wanted to open the car door and assure him that everything was fine and we could still be friends. Because we used to be friends. We really used to be something. Until it was set off course by all that violence, which of course was of no fault of our own. We were only kids. Playing. Laughing. Being immature.

Police lights worked off the sides of the houses, illuminating the siding and windows. Indicating emergency. But there were no sirens. Only two medics at the side window of Mr. Ellison's car asking me if they were able to open the door and check things out. As I nodded in agreement, the heavyset male medic with a Fu Manchu was already popping the handle and working the door open. It was stubborn, catching against a mound of dirt, but knowing the damage was already done, he ripped the door wide and knelt down beside me. The female medic noted Tarkin laying a little ways into the woods and began to head his way.

"Gonna need you to shut that engine down," said the medic with the Fu Manchu. "You okay? You feel alright?"

"Yeah," I said. "Yeah, go," motioning with my hand and nodding that he should go assist his partner with Adam. *Go save Adam.* But then came the thoughts of what he'd become and the concern of what he was capable of. And as I started to warn them, two more medics came to my aid and began an assessment of my vitals and mental status.

When they got me back up to the front of the house, they were loading Mrs. Tarkin into the back of an ambulance and another pulled away with Grandma Dar sitting up and showcased in the back square windows. She was clearly mumbling something to herself, but by all means seemed safe and healthy. Caroline sat on the tailgate of the fire chief's truck where a medic cleaned a cut on her forearm, and another tended to that wound around her ear. *She's clearly remarkable*, I thought to myself. *After all this, still in one piece.* Our eyes met and she went to stand, but the female medic did one of those *whoa, whoa, hey, hey's* and encouraged her to stay put. I walked up and threw my arms around her where we proceeded to cry beyond our years. It was a cry of survival and the guilt that goes along with. It was a cry that bound us. An assured vow beyond words.

"Don't forget my red, rosy ass," we heard a voice say.

We looked up to see David Trumner in all his glory. Hair tied back in a bit of a manbun. Tie-dyed shirt torn and dirty from his trek through the woods to get help. And in all that madness we'd forgotten what that meant. To be under the care of our local authorities. Authorities that he and Julie and her mother insisted come our way. He leaned his massive weight upon us, tossing an arm over both of our shoulders, and we hugged in a strange sort of victory. Not a victory like we'd won anything, though we'd escaped with our lives, but a strange semblance of something beyond understanding that only we were able to share.

"Shit, brother," I said. "It's so fuckin' good to see you."

"Is it really you?" Caroline asked, leaning back and taking his big, beautiful face into her hands.

Trumner's face rolled in on itself as an enormous smile populated his features and swelled him up good. "In the flesh," he nodded as we all sobbed and laughed.

An ambulance stopped in the middle of the street, and a medic with curly black hair and no undershirt beneath his uniform opened one of the side doors. My mom hopped down out of the vehicle and rushed over to squeeze me in her arms. *"You're alright. Thank God you're alright."*

"Dad?" I asked.

"He's good," she said, fighting back tears. "He's gonna be fine."

"Okay, go," I said. "We'll be right behind you." She brought a hand up to momentarily cup my cheek and stared at me, smiling. "Seriously, go. Be there soon." She planted a kiss on my forehead before grabbing Trumner's big, beautiful face in both hands and doing the same. When she approached Caroline, she did so a little more cautiously to avoid that ear before also planting a kiss on her forehead. And with that she stepped back up into the ambulance, taking the medic's offered hand and disappearing back inside. The driver gave a few cops leaning against their cruiser a *bleep* from the sirens, and the two waved without uncrossing their arms, hands coming up from the inner nooks of their elbows like little puppets.

"Julie?" Caroline asked Trumner.

"Total bitch the whole way into town, but she's fine. Resting easy with her mom at St. E's Edgewood."

"Hon," said the medic, working on rebandaging Caroline's wound. "I think we need to get you in soon. Nothing urgent but need a doc to look at this laceration." She brought the medical wrap beneath her jaw and up over the top of her head where she pinned it in place with little aluminum teeth. "Okay, I'm gonna tell them you'll roll back with us. Give you a few more minutes."

"Sounds good," Caroline said. "Thank you."

"You've got it, kiddo."

"She's good," Trumner said. "She's really good."

"Stop," I told him. "Not the time."

"I'm sayin' it seems like she fell into the right line of work is all. Nothing whatsoever to do with looks. Sure, she wears a uniform well, and I'm pretty sure I noticed a wing or the pointy lettering of a sleeve tattoo, which I find insanely attractive, but my focus here is on her dedication to the occupation. Nothing more."

"I'm glad to see you're still an idiot, buddy."

"Oh, me too," he said. And then his eyes just sort of got sad. Saying, without saying, *our laughter won't come as easy. Not anymore. Not like it used to. Not without the rest of us. Sure, we'll eventually move on and find happiness, but there will always be an empty spot. Our very own sorrow. And that's fine. To be expected, honestly. The only way you can genuinely honor someone is to ensure a little piece of you dies along with them. And I know that sounds silly, but Kemper, Bently, Dufour, those guys deserved it. They deserved that at least. So, okay, we'll be sad. Not always, but forever. And we'll be happy too, not always, but forever.*

An overweight police officer nonchalantly popped his trunk and began fencing off the Ellisons' front yard and driveway, weaving yellow cautionary tape between the mailbox and a few stakes they stamped into the yard. News vans fell in line near the front entrance of the neighborhood. Cameramen paratrooped from side doors, like angry Dreadknocks. Sheriff Sumpter walked up to the line where another officer was keeping them at bay. The three of us watched as the estuary of a microphone was pressed so close to his face that he nearly went cross-eyed. On the other end, was a young woman with impulsively white teeth and skin decimated by self-tanner. She wore an outfit one might wear to a benefit or ribbon cutting ceremony, sort of thing that played nicely on a television screen. She was moderately pretty, but mostly a mess.

"Sheriff," she began. "Can you tell us the number of victims?"

"No," Sheriff Sumpter said, taking the microphone into his hands and causing the reporter to sort of pull back on it like a jet pilot.

"*That's okay,*" she said. "*I'll hold it. I'll hold it for you.*"

"*Ah,*" he responded. "Very good."

She went all game-faced and repositioned so that just beyond her shoulder were the necessary elements of tragedy. "Good?" she asked the cameraman as he arranged the rocket launcher-sized camera on his shoulder and tweaked the lens before thumbing a *good to go*. And then things went to chaos. Light clicked on over the hill, behind the Tarkins' house, as a female voice screamed over and over like the chorus from some demented song, *No! No! No!* The medic who tended to Caroline rushed toward the side of the house, fashioning a tourniquet to stall blood. When we finally saw the medic who assisted me from the car, she was walking on bone. Foot torn from ankle, pegleg of the most painful kind. Fingers dangling from thin lines of skin like spit hanging off lip, before snapping loose and down into the grass. By the way the others hollered up from behind the house, I knew without looking that the other medic was gone.

"*Tarkin,*" I said to no one in particular, but he didn't appear. More medics went around the back of the house where the light had gone out. We waited in silence, unable to put into words what they were walking into, as the front door of the house creaked open. Three officers stepped into the front yard and drew their weapons; arms slightly bent in anticipation of shots they never thought they'd fire. And from out of the darkness, the frail body of Adam Tarkin began to emerge. The opposite of something sinking, instead surfacing and coming to form. He walked slowly, dragging his left side in his wake. Sounds of metal scraping wood.

"*Put the gun down, son,*" one of the officers said, though I was uncertain as to which and it hardly mattered. But they didn't know the history. Didn't realize that some things happen without explanation. Following the officer's request, Tarkin simply sat down in one of the two rocking chairs on the front porch. Same ones Kemper and I used to sit in waiting for him to bring us popsicles, finish dinner, or change his clothes. The officers began saying things like *Now take it easy, it's gonna be okay* and *There's a way out of this*. And that last one was almost comical. A perfect stranger, having no knowledge of what played out in our tiny little neighborhood on a random Friday night, having the gall to tell Adam Tarkin there was a way out. And though I'm not certain if it was Adam Tarkin or Calm Jeffrey who placed those barrels beneath his chin, I'd like to believe that the way out was instantaneous, void of pain, an erasure of memory and blame. Concrete proof that there were only victims that night, and Adam Tarkin should be counted among them. And right then I promised Adam that I would clear his name. To the best of my ability, I would inform those who were not there that he was innocent. No matter the cost. As long as my body held breath, I promised him I would.

EPILOGUE: A PROMISE...IS A PROMISE...IS A PROMISE...

David Trumner's heart went splits on a Thursday evening following *Nina's Goodnight Show* on Sprout. As was their routine, he sat with his three-year-old daughter, Sadie, who snuggled against him on the couch and watched their regularly scheduled program. A program consisting of *The Berenstain Bears, Caillou, Angelina Ballerina,* and *Pajanimals.* Shortly thereafter, he scooped Sadie up into his massive arms and projected her up above his head with her back flush against the ceiling, flying as a superhero might. And as always, his wife, Vanessa, said, "*Don't get her riled up before bed, David,*" secretly loving the simplicity and playfulness of their nightly routine. I know all this because Vanessa called me shortly after he was pronounced. Going through the residual guilt that comes with sudden loss. Wondering if she'd missed signs. Or maybe she should have just stayed up and watched Thursday Night Football with him. Perhaps there was something she could have done? But a widow maker is stealthy in its pursuits, and its destruction is often irrefutable.

He was twenty-seven years old.

We left the following morning. Loading up Aubby and all her non-negotiables, mainly consisting of her pumpkin pajamas, which she wore all year round, and Scapegoat and Planter, stuffed animals she'd slept with since she was a baby. The first being exactly as one might assume, a billy goat, and the other a gray bunny rabbit with a plush carrot wedged between its paws. Both worn thin of fabric by way of continuous affection. When I went to collect them that morning, Scapegoat was wedged beneath the bulk of a pillow as though squashed by a falling boulder. Only his muzzle and tassel visible. Planter was nothing more than two gray ears breaching the surface of the comforter. They both smelled of her, that enmeshed odor of youth and saliva. Soft little souls she cuddled up with each night. I sat on the edge of her bed and thought about David's daughter, Sadie, and how such sadness would steal a portion of her childhood.

On Aubby's bedside table sat one of those tiny projectors that played hushed versions of nursery rhymes and splayed images upon the ceiling. Humpty Dumpty, the cow jumping over the moon, and an assortment of other fabled characters. I turned it on and sat on the bed. Each evening, as was our routine, Aubby and I lay in bed staring up at those images, whispering in each other's ears, until sleep came for us. Feeling so safe in our sacred little world. Our ritual. Our little life. I moved a hand over the lens of the projector, chopping through the light. A miniature version of Jack and Jill rotated upon the landscape of my palm until I closed them down inside the machine and pulled the plug from the wall.

The road trip was roughly eight hours from Wrightsville, North Carolina to the small Northern Kentucky city of Upper Hearth, but when a friend falls, you go. You always go. And as much as Caroline and I swore never to return, our loyalty insisted.

Much of the trip was filled with music and laughter. We listened to a podcast that was way more interesting than I would have thought based on its title referencing a town of feces, but the dread of our return remained.

Sitting in the back corners of our brains. Surfacing each time our minds were not occupied. Resurrecting visions of that night ten years ago. Or, not just visions of that night, but memories of Kemper and Bently, Dufour and even Julie. Fun times. Times before things got sad. But mostly Trumner. Afterall, he was the reason we were heading back, to give him the proper send off. The one he deserved.

Caroline and Julie had a falling out years prior. It was inevitable, in all honesty. Their moral compasses simply wouldn't align. Not to mention her mother's pursuits with Mrs. Tarkin, suing her in civil court and badmouthing her around town. And sure, there were some terrible things that had taken place that night, but what Julie and her mother suffered were not among the most reprehensible. Not to mention, Julie knew what happened with the Tarkin's was completely beyond their control. Made no matter. Some people don't want the truth. Not when there might be a little money or attention to be sought. Caroline caught Julie at a party in our early twenties talking poorly about Kemper and building herself up as a survivor. One of the few who didn't become one of Adam Tarkin's victims. She never told me what was said and I didn't pursue it much further. It hardly mattered. Once a wolf shows you its teeth, you hardly notice its smile.

Years later, not long after we married and bought our house, I caught Caroline in the office drinking wine and playing a solo round of *Futures! Futures! Futures!* I grabbed a beer and leaned against the desk as she read aloud. Now, mind you, my wife is the sweetest person I know and would do absolutely anything for nearly anyone, but Julie crossed the line and a toll needed to be paid. Above Julie's senior picture it simply read, "Julie Derringer, a cunt of such exorbitant proportions that she awoke one morning to look in the mirror and see one enormous cunt."

We arrived in Upper Hearth just before dinnertime and decided to take Aubby to Knuck 'n Futz for some wings, and those potato rounds kids can order with the smiley faces on them. Caroline and I each ordered a beer and sat in a bit of disbelief that we were home. Such a strange feeling, knowing that we were sitting just five minutes down the road from where we once went through hell. Literal hell. One that took our friends and neighbors and destroyed our innocence. From what we learned, every last resident had moved out of the old neighborhood. There were rumors that those who stayed began seeing shadows. Police officers were called out at odd hours to investigate when people began seeing dead relatives, classmates, and historical town figures, but nothing much came of it. Only answer was to move. And so, they did. Family after family. Home after home. Abandoned. And left to rot.

Our hotel was just off the I-275 loop on the Wilder Exit, but I found myself pulled toward our old neighborhood. Felt a need to see for myself. And when I turned away from the highway and looked to Caroline, she simply nodded in agreement, that we should go have a look. Aubby sat in the back kicking her legs and singing a song from one of the many Disney movies I'd fallen asleep watching with her. She was a trooper, only getting cranky on one occasion during the ride when she couldn't get her crayon box open. Other than that, she was a total angel. She asked, "What's this place?" when we pulled past the stone wall reading *Georgetown Village*, the light which once shined up from the ground long since covered by kudzu.

"*This*," I began, "is where I met your beautiful mother, sweetie."

She leaned up out of her seat, and I told her she could unbuckle. We made our way past Tarkin's and Kemper's houses without the courage to so much as look in their direction. There was no fear then, just the triggering worry of memories. When we passed the stretch of fenceline by the Bartletts', I pulled to a bit of a stop. "Right there, that little alleyway, that's where your mom held my hand for the first time. She was so in love with me."

"It's true. Your father used to be quite handsome."

I responded by doing that open-mouthed look of shock and Aubby said, without skipping a beat, *"And he used to have hair!"*

"Why I oughta," I said, reaching blindly behind my seat to tickle her legs.

We then headed down to the end of the street where my old house sat. The one I was lucky enough to share with Grandma Dar. The one that contained such pure memories, at least, until it didn't. Sometimes things happen of such significance that a place loses all capability to contain positive memories. Even the good ones are tarnished, unable to shine.

"See that one, right there?" I said.

"Uh huh," she responded, nodding her head and stretching her neck to see out the side window.

"That's where I grew up with Nana and Papaw and your Great-Grandma Dar. You never got to meet her on account of her needing to be in Heaven, but you would have loved her, and she would have loved you. She was the best."

"Was she tall?" Aubby asked. "Because I wanna be tall."

"She was," I told her. "But then she started shrinking."

"Wait," she asked. "People shrink? Like laundry?"

We all laughed and Caroline explained that the luckiest people do. "They shrink from this life and grow tall in the next."

"That sounds nice," Aubby said. And we let it be.

Sunlight was beginning to fade, so we decided it best to go check into our hotel, but as we neared the front of the neighborhood, we noted a white Dodge Ram coming our way. But just before it reached us, it pulled into Adam Tarkin's old driveway. A man stepped out and began walking down toward the street to greet us. He was handsome and looked to be in control of his decisions, wearing a button-down that was likely overpriced and pair of Chinos. He smiled and raised a hand that we should stop.

"Evening," he said. And for reasons I can't quite explain, I didn't respond.

"Oh, hi," Caroline said. "How are you?"

"Fine," he said. "Just fine. Not used to seeing folks in this neighborhood."

"We were just headin' out," I said and began to roll my window up.

"*Oh, sorry,*" he said, placing a hand on the door frame. "Was hardly tryin' to scare you off." When I looked at his hand, he noted my discomfort and stepped away from the vehicle. "I've just been coming around the past few weeks and have yet to see a soul was all I meant. Anyway, my name's Andy George and I'm a documentary filmmaker. Or, sorry, scratch that. An aspiring documentary filmmaker. Have an aim to make a film about what took place here years back. Or, at least, what some folks claim to have taken place. You know anything about all that? Can hardly get anyone to talk about it. The subject's taboo."

I stared right through Andy George, wanting no part of what he was asking about, and then looked over at Caroline who, as was still a natural habit, brought her hair back and tucked it behind an ear missing its lobe, with that white raised scar along her jawline. When my attention returned to the man, he clearly understood our history, as though some hushed voice was whispering to him, "*They know. They were here. They know everything.*"

"Sorry, we're just in from North Carolina and doing a bit of exploring."

"*Ah,*" he said with doubt in his eyes. "I understand. You all have a good evening."

"You do the same," Caroline said, as I brought the window up and pulled away from the curb. And as I watched the man head back up the driveway in my rearview, I heard that same voice in my head, promising Adam Tarkin that I'd clear his name. Promising that I would tell anyone who would listen that he was not the monster they claimed him to be. And without being fully aware I was doing so, I applied the brakes and threw the car in reverse. Andy George took note and headed back toward the curb. Walking slowly. As one might when approaching an unfamiliar animal. Unaware of the story he was about to hear. One of shadow, friendship, love, and loss. The one that made me who I am today.

THE END

ACKNOWLEDGMENTS

This idea had been running around in my head for a number of years when I finally presented it to our oldest daughter, Addie. We were sitting on the back deck on a beautiful summer evening when I told her about a group of teens getting together in a pot circle after word spread that their classmate was going to have an exorcism. After I enthusiastically acted out the scenario, Addie surprised me by saying, "That's really good, dad. I'd watch that movie." When I responded by asking if she'd read the book she said, "*Yeah, uh, no.*" But the fact that a fifteen-year-old girl could visualize my story and liked it, well that made me start to believe. Subsequently, her sister Norah, who was only twelve at the time, had become obsessed with the movie Dazed and Confused. *I know, I know,* bad parenting, letting our daughter watch that one at such a young age, but after further consideration, I began to see past the drinking and drugs and started honing in on what really made that movie special...the relationships. I decided then and there that I wanted the teens in this work to have that same sort of comradery and love for one another. I hope I did them justice.

I would also like to thank Tony Anuci of Anuci Press for seeing the potential of this story. And thankfully, unlike Addie, being interested in reading the book! And here you have it. The book, alive and well in the world. Hope you enjoyed it. Hope it scared you a little. And most importantly, I hope you cared about Bauschy, Caroline, Kemper, Trumner and of course Adam Tarkin, the head case, the tragic soul...*the possessed boy.*

Special thanks to Darin Overholser for his incredible book cover design. He absolutely crushed it!

And, as always, I'd like to thank my beautiful wife, Marlayna, for all her support and allowing me to still pursue this dream. She takes on so much for our family and allows me time to write, believes in my ideas and lets me still be a bit of a child from time to time.

www.ingramcontent.com/pod-product-compliance
Lightning Source LLC
Chambersburg PA
CBHW071739150726
47998CB00005B/1719